MY  402272
14.95
Orenstein Aug87
A candidate for murder

DATE DUE			

GREAT RIVER REGIONAL LIBRARY
St. Cloud, Minnesota 56301

A CANDIDATE FOR MURDER

Also by Frank Orenstein:
Murder on Madison Avenue
The Man in the Gray Flannel Shroud

A CANDIDATE FOR MURDER

An Ev Franklin Mystery

Frank Orenstein

ST. MARTIN'S PRESS
NEW YORK

A CANDIDATE FOR MURDER. Copyright © 1987 by Frank Orenstein. All rights reserved. Printed in the United States of America. No part of this book may be used or reproduced in any manner whatsoever without written permission except in the case of brief quotations embodied in critical articles or reviews. For information, address St. Martin's Press, 175 Fifth Avenue, New York, N.Y. 10010.

Library of Congress Cataloging-in-Publication Data

Orenstein, Frank.
    A candidate for murder.

"A Thomas Dunne Book"
I. Title.
PS3565.R39C36   1987   813'.54   87-4449
ISBN 0-312-00572-5

First Edition
10 9 8 7 6 5 4 3 2 1

For sibs and peers:
Etta and Harold; Ruth and Shy

ONE

Four o'clock of a rainy predawn, all flights delayed. Porters drift trancelike, emptying ashtrays, shuffling, yawning. None here but the undead, men needing shaves, women with hair in strings and mascara on the run; an empassioned nose-picker the only sign of life. The servicemen alone, stretched out across molded plastic seats and sleeping as only servicemen can sleep, were at peace. The rest of us floated aimlessly, staring through the grilles of darkened gift shops filled with teddy bears, fun hats, and other souvenirs even shoddier than the places they were intended to commemorate, reading yesterday's headlines, pacing and pacing and praying for our flights to arrive.

I found a nominally functioning cafeteria dispensing the previous day's bitter coffee and a limited assortment of stale sweet rolls, all served on chipped, yellowed china. I covered a coffee-stained plate with what purported to be a cherry danish, though the red blob at its center looked more like the bloodshot eye of a long dead sea monster, cold, clammy, and viscous. Slapping my catch onto a table, I slid into the bolted-to-the-floor seat. The danish glared malevolently, and I returned the compliment. We sat considering each other venomously, neither of us sufficiently enspirited for truly active aggression. I suddenly knew I had no intention of biting into the loathsome beast, and it in turn was too ancient and sodden to attempt a frontal attack of its own.

One sip of the brew was enough, though it was blessedly too hot for its full acidity to come through. I pushed my goodies aside to search for a bar. I found one. It was closed. I was limited to staring into the dark to spot those bottles that infest the bars in every airport on earth—ouzo, cherry heering, chocolate mint liqueur, and sundry other depressants.

Finding a seat miraculously unencumbered of a serviceman, I sagged into it, easing aside the army boots that were crowding in from the corpse across the three positions to my left and contemplated my situation. I had resisted this out-of-town assignment from my employers at a New York advertising agency to develop a public opinion polling program for a political candidate, our newest client, but had nevertheless been sent forth. Ed Jorgensen, head honcho of the pearl of Madison Avenue, Finch, Rowan, & Hyde, advertisers to the elite and anybody else with cash, was not to be denied. At least not by a mere employee. Only by Mrs. Jorgensen. Maybe.

Once I was out in the field, here in Iowa, the same potentate, Tsar Edward the First (and, I hoped, the last), had summoned me back peremptorily for what he decided was urgent business in New York. Wherever you are, agency presidents figure they need you someplace else, which accounted for my predawn presence at the airport.

Events had moved at a less than stately pace during my four days in Iowa. The client, no seamier than most politicians, had been attacked twice with lethal weapons. Guns. The first attack had clearly been intended to usher him out of the political arena on a permanent and irreversible basis. The goal of the second attack had either been meant to kill or had not been meant to kill; it wasn't clear which. I had a sinking feeling that before this campaign was over I would have had several too many opportunities to find out which, opportunities I would fear, resist, try to fend off, or at least weasel out of, all to no avail.

The whole mess had started just a couple of weeks earlier.

TWO

The phone rang. Sally Turner, my secretary, answered it and bawled in to me, "Himself wants you in his office. Chop chop."

"What about?" I yelled back.

She appeared in the doorway and yawned. "Who knows? Yours not to reason why, Ev. You know that," she added reprovingly.

She was right. I left my eleventh floor office, the one that read Everett Franklin, VP Research, on the door, and hustled up to the more rarefied heavens of the thirtieth floor and the office of the president, Ed Jorgensen. That's when I found out that my new assignment would be doing political opinion polling.

I didn't want to work for the candidate, not because I had anything against him, but because public opinion polling for office seekers has reached the point of lunacy. Most hungry politicians stand on two-legged platforms these days. The first leg is whatever the big-money contributors want it to be and the second is whatever the pollsters say the voters want it to be. But anybody who has taken a high school physics class knows that a stool needs a minimum of three legs to stand. In this case, oh, radical notion! the third one might well have been what the candidate himself thought appropriate to the needs of the country, but I suppose such an approach to politics is too old-fashioned.

But Finch, Rowan, & Hyde didn't concern itself with the unrealistic niceties. They had landed the account by selling the man what we call an integrated package—advertising campaign, public relations campaign, and frequent public opinion polling to find out if the voters were dancing appropriately to all that jazz and to provide feedback for further razzmatazz.

Sounds good, integrated package, doesn't it? Can't you just see the sales pitch to the prospective client? "Slide 1: An Integrated Package to Make Mayor John McGrath . . . Slide 2: *The People's Choice!*" (Background of ballot boxes, cheering crowds, and, natch, the White House. Matching sound effects cued in by computer-controlled and -programmed system.)

That's the way the world goes, and a lot of us must like it. It's popular wisdom that if Richard Nixon had covered up his five o'clock shadow with rice powder so that he looked more like a Kabuki dancer than a second-story man when he debated clean-cut Jack Kennedy, he might have moved the wife and kids into the White House a couple of terms earlier than he did. We like our candidates squeaky clean, at least on the outside, just like our hair and our shirt collars.

Of course I squawked when Big Ed told me what the job was. "Damn it all, Ed, he ought to have a polling organization full time on the job! How can I see a campaign through, with the other work I've got? Besides, I do surveys on dog food. Public opinion polling is different."

"How?" he asked, quite reasonably. "It's only asking people what they want and don't want, no? That's what you've always said yourself, boy. So this time you'll be asking if they'll buy the dog instead of the dog food. What's the difference?"

He had me. There wasn't any difference, not enough to matter, anyway. I shifted the attack. "But what about the time away from the office? I can't afford it. The place'll go to hell."

He shook his head. "No, Ev, I don't think so. You'll have Jane to run things, right?" Jane was my highly competent assistant and my highly competent wife, not necessarily in that order.

"Yeah, but she'll have my work on top of her own, and maybe that'd work for three, four weeks, but she'd drown in it after that."

He had me again, this time in spades with whipped cream and a cherry on top. "Fine!" he said first. Then he added, "I'm glad you agree." His third and last remark was, "That's settled, then."

"Oh?" I asked. "Well, in the order in which you bring it up, first, what makes you think so? Second, do I? And third, is it?"

A mosquito never troubles an elephant, especially when the elephant has the keys to the safe. He laughed, amused, I presume, at my presumption. "You'll see," he promised. "We're having lunch with Al Delaney, McGrath's campaign manager. I'll fill you in first."

The gist was that there were three of us assigned to work with the candidate: a pollster, me, to tell him whether he was in favor of increasing Social Security pensions or shooting everybody over seventy or letting them starve to death so that a special commission could announce subsequently that there was no hunger in America; an account executive, whose functions I have never understood myself beyond his ability to carry messages back and forth between the client and the copywriters and artists, look beautiful, and see to it that the client's coffee is ready, hot, and contains the requisite doses of cream and sugar; and a public relations man, whose job is more complex and can best be explained by illustration. A routine P.R. man will arrange for a candidate to kiss orphans in urban slums, milk cows in Wisconsin, ride subways in New York, and march in St. Patrick's Day parades anywhere. A smart one does better. Do you remember the black presidential candidate who made some remarks offensive to the Jewish vote? He squirmed on the end of the hook for a while, and finally went to a local synagogue to apologize. Just dandy, as far as it went, but a top notch P.R. man would have had him go to the synagogue, apologize, and then, with a battery of television cameras grinding, do the windows.

That's the kind of savvy Finch, Rowan, & Hyde could provide. And in case you think I'm being cynical and even tasteless, don't take my word for it, but gum on this for a moment, quoted directly from the Voice of Destiny, otherwise known as *The New York Times*. In an article about an incumbent president's plans for reelection, the *Times* had it that, "The president's campaign aides speak admiringly of the warmth, the vitality, and good feeling conveyed so artfully in Pepsi-Cola and beer commercials. The talents which lie behind such products line Madison Avenue." And that, they explained, is why the president decided to bring "... his needs ... to Manhattan, like Procter & Gamble with a commercial product line to merchandise ..."*

And that's how I got to be John McGrath's pollster, taking him on as another one of my assignments, like testing consumer reactions to deodorants, laxatives, and acne creams. Mayor John McGrath—Johnny to you, if you've

---

**The New York Times*, March 4, 1984.

got a vote—was after his party's nomination for the presidency of that nation which every four years gets pluralized into "these United States of America," as opposed, I imagine, to those United States of America or even to them U.S. of A.

Johnny, as I was to learn later, had some major assets: he sprang from a heartland rural state, and had become mayor of a town whose privacy I will respect by saying only that its name causes the heart to leap skyward as joyfully as if it had been dubbed Frozen Meat Loaf, North Columbiana. His other assets included relative youthfulness—he was still under fifty—and a blow dry hair job, both of which would appeal to young voters. His handicaps included relative youthfulness—still under fifty—and a blow dry hair job, both of which would appeal to young voters, who don't turn out on election day like their elders. The fact that all-American, grass roots, heartland states like North Columbiana have as many electoral votes as you can count on the hooves of ten beef cattle wasn't overly advantageous either.

But John McGrath was nobody's nudnik: He didn't *want* the nomination, not really. He only wanted to try for it and miss. The other party's candidate was just concluding a successful first term as chief of state. The country was prosperous and technically not at war, no matter how fast and hot the words and bullets were flying at half a dozen places around the world. Furthermore the incumbent had let us simple folk know that the Almighty had already lined up behind his administration. He was a cinch for reelection.

No, what Johnny wanted was to lose the party nomination. Lose, but come in a strong second, so that the first place patsy would get stuck with the bad news label when he lost the big one to the incumbent. McGrath would become a major power broker in the party after that, unencumbered by responsibility for its failures. Then, in another four years, still relatively youthful, and as blow-dried as the fashion of the times might decree, he'd be in a position to take over and win the nomination. Meanwhile, he'd have had those years to build up what our more customary clients on Madison Avenue call positive name recognition, the presumed impulse on the part of a consumer to tear off a piece and eat, tip the bottle and gargle, or dab sparingly on the pulse points.

And if Finch, Rowan, & Hyde brought it off, got the scenario, as we call it, to work as planned, what a plum it would be—advertising agents to presidents, like corsetieres by appointment to the queen.

That was the story I got from Big Ed Jorgensen, who then gave me ten minutes to tidy up for fingernail inspection before lunch with Al Delaney.

Delaney was a florid chappie, both personally and professionally friendly, outgoing, and given to positive thinking. Other than that he was very much like me, about forty-five or so, with brown eyes and hair, and the faintest hint of being about to give birth to a paunch. He was nearer to it than I was, thanks to Jane's putting me on occasional torture diets of organically grown grass with raspberry vinegar, imitation margarine on gluten bread, and quick-frozen shreds of tofu-flavored cardboard substitute. Delaney sipped his drinks appreciatively but with delicacy and direction, evincing the single-minded determination of a man who isn't sure about the provenance of his next pink lady, should the home team happen to lose. We talked about the first contest for the party's nomination, the one in Iowa. "Johnny can handle Iowa himself," he informed us. "We won't need you people there and we want to hang onto our cash for later, when we will need it. The university kids are working for him, and they'll be doing the opinion polls under a marketing professor. That's all we'll need; maybe we could use more, but we'll settle for that right now."

"I understand," Ed said, "but you ought to have some of our people go out and get acquainted with Johnny, get to know his style, get a feel for how we're going to work with you."

"That's fine, so long as you understand we're not running hard and expensive out there. Johnny'll get his second-place finish without it. He starts with a good edge—rural, midwest background. Small town virtues. That stuff." He described a few small circles with his hand. "They're him, the voters in Iowa, and he's them. We'll take our chances with them.

"All right," he went on, "so Iowa's first. We'll do fine. Nothing splashy, but okay. What we want Finch, Rowan, & Hyde to concentrate on is the next test, New Hampshire. We need a close second, at least, out of a field of eight guys making a grab for the gold ring, and maybe, just maybe, a first. Hell, we know he doesn't get the nomination this time, but the party'll sit up and pay attention if he takes a state in the East, and then puts himself over in the South. The big boys still won't buy, and we don't want them to, but in four years he'll have something to sell, and we're gonna make them hot for it."

"We'll do it," Jorgensen said. "We've got the best there is in Finch, Rowan, & Hyde. Ev here's the top man in the opinion field and he'll tell your man what's going to get those voters to stand up and salute." Ed was a man of taste, and hence not given to exaggeration; he was only lying with conviction, like a good ad man should. "Bill Toscani's your account man. He'll be in constant touch with the crews that turn out the copy and the commercials and package what the candidate wants to say in the way the people want him to say it. You see the commercials running now for Chomps dog food?"

Delaney looked glazed. "I don't think so. We've got this cat."

"Well, anyway, Toscani masterminded that campaign. Took every prize in the industry, and topped the Relative Sales Conviction field tests in six major metropolitan areas. For P.R. you'll have Betty Gold, and she'll get you all the media coverage your man can stand up to, whatever way is best, from tapping maple syrup—"

"Maple syrup gets itself tapped in the spring, Ed," I interjected, just to dilute the bull.

"—from tapping maple syrup, if that's what your man wants," the elephant went on, brushing off us mosquitoes, "to quarrying New Hampshire granite, unless that only gets tapped in the spring too."

"It'll be ready for tapping whenever you say. You too, Al," I added.

"That's the spirit," Jorgensen said. Delaney laughed. I couldn't imagine why.

Suddenly I knew how I had dug a hole and jumped into it in Big Ed's office. This job, at least to begin with, out in Iowa, would take me away from the office for far less than the three or four weeks I had said was feasible. Damn it! Eight candidates, and I had to work on making our man Snow White and the others into the seven dwarfs. And it didn't even occur to me that there was to be a wicked queen in the same story.

THREE

I came to two conclusions about Johnny McGrath almost immediately: He wasn't a bad guy, and I didn't like him all that much. I felt like something being mauled into shape on an assembly line as he pumped my extended paw earnestly, saying "Good to meet ya, fella!" and then propelled me to the next processing position so he could get on with meeting more little people with equal sincerity. I got the notion that if there had been a trash compactor waiting for me to step into, Johnny would have found it as convenient as it might have been regrettable.

I was a cog, I told myself. Johnny had to talk to an infinity of people each day, each of whom had a hand to be shaken, kissed, or licked. He couldn't treat people as if they really existed. I still didn't like it, even after lecturing myself, but the pay was good.

"Sit, sit," he urged Betty Gold, Bill Toscani, and me on our arrival at his hotel in Des Moines. "Let's go over the game plan." He grinned warmly, and I knew that Bill was already dreaming up commercial angles to highlight those many sincere and flashing teeth. Johnny was tall and lean, with arms that hung too far out of his sleeves, making him either Lincolnesque or apelike, depending on your political sympathies. A lock of chestnut hair fell over his forehead with calculated carelessness, and something told me that if this guy ever got to be president there'd be stories about the cost of flying his personal hairburner around the world on Air Force One, the way reporters with nothing more important to do used to niggle at the cost of transporting Antoine for the wives of earlier presidents.

"I want you three to get a sense of my style, what I've got to say and how I say it. There's nothing you can do for me in Iowa, but it'll give you a running start for New Hampshire. That's where I'm going to work your butts off. You understand? So enjoy yourselves while you can." There was no boyish grin left. The rawboned country look had turned into big city steel—polished, hard, and cold. "Now, are there any questions?"

"Just one," Bill Toscani said. "What I don't understand is why you're settling for second. Why not first? With Finch, Rowan, & Hyde on the team, why not try to take it all? It's a matter of image, Johnny, and image-making is what we're all about." Trust an account man to make a pitch for a client to spend more money, even when it made no sense at all, and trust an account man not to understand the basic strategy when it involves something more complicated than a snappy slogan to pull one brand of detergent out in front of its identical twin. Betty Gold studied a spot on the carpet, while I trained my eyes onto a parking lot outside the window. I cringed.

McGrath's eyes were glued on poor Bill, and they sent out sparks. "Ed," he said firmly, "or is it Bill. Bill then.

There are two things you've got to learn if we're going to get along. The first is that I am in no way a box of cereal, and the second is that I am definitely in no way a box of cereal. You keep that straight and we're okay. You work on this image shit. Fine. But I set the strategy. You work within the confines of what I want to accomplish. Period."

He got up and started pacing, long legs kicking out from the knees, as if Toscani's head was a soccer ball in his path. Stopping, he wagged a finger. "You ought to know, you three, that I think I need you and that I'm sorry as hell about that. I want to get a fix on what the public is concerned about, and then I'll tell them in my way, in my own way, what my point of view is. You figure out how my message comes across, if they understand me, if I'm putting anybody off. You can help me improve it, but basically it's going to be me talking. There's not going to be any wind-up dummy for your bunch to hang Christmas tree balls on. Is that clear to everybody?"

We three, the most of Madison Avenue, mumbled agreement in tiny voices. I thought I might even develop some grudging respect for the candidate—if I could believe what he said, which I wasn't sure I could. These guys are always on stage. I also thought I might just hammer on Toscani's thick head for getting us lectured at like this, and so late in life.

"I'll tell you what," the candidate said, simmering down, "we'll talk more tomorrow, but I've got to get ready now for the debate tonight. You'll get a look at the opposition for yourselves. Dick Havemeyer is going to get the nomination. You can catch his act. He's been governor of his sate, had two terms in the House, and a stretch as secretary of agriculture the last time the party was in. He's got something for everyone, the bastard, and he's done something, even if not very much, for everyone, and now he's calling in the chips.

"The ones we've got to nose out are Bobby Leich and

Vern Duckworth. Pardon me, the Reverend Vernon Duckworth," he said with mock respect, the words coming out of a twisted mouth.

I wondered what was going on when candidates for high office had gone so damn folksy: Johnny, Bobby, Dick, Vern. What would happen if an office-seeker said to the voters, "No, you may not call me Franky. Franklin Delano is the name." Would we have had the poor sap guillotined?

"Johnny," I urged, "give us another couple of seconds, okay? What do we look for tonight? What makes Bobby Leich and Vern Duckworth the ones to beat?"

"Okay." He thought for a moment, an attractive frown creasing that manly brow. "Leich and I are both after the vote that doesn't come from the traditional party backers. The young. The not too liberal liberals. The women who are mad as hell at the way they figure we've taken them for granted. The minorities, whether racial, ethnic, or, God help us, even sexual. The party mainstream is tired, and they don't know whether they're supporting Dick Havemeyer or Benjamin Harrison. Some of them don't even care. They're with us because they've got no place else to go. If Leich or I can stir them up, we'll grab off a good chunk of support, but Leich's got a big head start; he's been a national figure for ten years and he's not going to let anybody forget it.

"Now the Right Reverend Vernon Duckworth is something else again. Essentially he's a one issue candidate, but when he's taken an option on God, he's got a good thing going. Personally, if there was a way to keep him from getting the nomination I'd grab it even if it meant my losing. The son of a bitch has preempted the Lord: If you don't like drugs, abortion, foreigners, atheists, big unions, big corporations—hell! anybody who isn't you—vote for Duckworth and God. In that order. He started out as a revivalist in Texas, pitching tents for Jesus and getting the crowds to pitch pennies for Duckworth. But you know that already, I'm sure. He's a mean little man. I used to think he had dollar signs in those piggy eyes, but that underrates him. Now I think he wants power, but he doesn't know what for. He'll figure it out when he gets there; the Lord'll give him a couple of tips. He may even be almost honest about it, and that's not the least of what scares me about the man. He's a big, negative howl about a disintegrating world, and the howl raises an echo out there."

He stopped. "That's enough about Vern Duckworth. I could go on for days. The others are nothing to worry about. They're the one issue types, too, but dull issues like disarmament, the environment, minority rights. They've got their constituencies, but they're too narrowly based to make it. They know it—they're no fools—but they're out to make a point. Like Pete Montano, who's running on unilateral nuclear disarmament. He's going but nowhere, but if he gets ten percent of the delegates he can make the party listen. Montano's a good man. Honest. But a loser. Too honest is death, like too dishonest. A little of each is what makes a winner."

He grinned. "That's what you three are here for. I'll take care of the honest bit, and you can handle the rest. Now I've got to get going. See you at the debate. Get yourselves into Al Delaney's suite this afternoon and meet the rest of the crowd. Good to have you aboard." He whipped out. A paper fluttered off the coffee table in his wake.

"Wow," Betty said. "He's sexy. We can do a lot with him."

"Yeah?" I asked, "Well, you play it cool, dolly. Don't get any ideas that he can do a lot with you, you hear?"

"Not to worry," Betty said. "These days me thinking about sex is like reading recipes in the Sunday paper. There comes a time when a girl knows she's never going to sample it all, no matter how yummy it looks, so there's no use in tearing it out to try later." Betty was a former femme fatale now in her upper thirties, still attractive, but looking a bit tired, and on the verge of pushing curvaceousness past the point of no return. She was, in short, partially burned out, but with some smoking timbers not without appeal remaining in situ. There was a Mr. Gold somewhere, but office rumor had it that he was filed under things to do on a rainy day, along with instructions on how to build an Eiffel Tower out of matchsticks.

But don't get me wrong. Betty wasn't promiscuous. She was notoriously true to one guy at a time, even if it wasn't necessarily the one she was married to. I loved her: She had had a ball and she didn't regret it. If she was sorry it was almost over, *almost* over, it was only with a happy wistfulness.

"Anyway," she went on, "I don't think I'd enjoy making it with young Abe Lincoln, if you want the truth. I'd never know if it was my body or my vote he was after. Even if I do have more body than vote these days. Let's get some lunch. Talking about it makes me almost as hungry these days as doing it used to."

"Listen," Toscani interrupted, "what's this line of his about us handling the dishonest bit? What's he think we are?"

"He doesn't think," I explained. "He knows." I patted Betty on the behind to move her forward. "Let's eat."

She patted me back, and we sallied forth to find some food.

FOUR

That afternoon Delaney introduced us to the campaign staff. I spent my time with Bob Glenn, the marketing professor who was running McGrath's local polling effort.

"They don't know the man around here," Glenn told me, "but they like him. Take a look at these results." He gestured toward a sheaf of computer printouts. "We finished the analysis this morning. McGrath comes from country like this, and folks out here think that's right neighborly of him. Automatically. You ask what his stand is on anything at all, and they don't know. But ask them if they approve of his stand on the same damn thing, and hell, yes, they approve in spades. They like the man, so his stand must be good, like old Uncle Bill down at the feed store on Railroad Street. A beauty contest, that's all it is. Anyway, you look this stuff over. I think you'll agree with me that the candidate better get some ideas out front before he sticks his nose on the other side of the Appalachians. Nobody back East is going to love him because he's young Lochinvar, if you know what I mean."

"I getcha," I said. "In my world we call it no brand name recognition. Maybe a little good will, but nothing for him, nothing against him. Can we go through some of this together? You got the time?"

He led me through three weeks of surveys, and I saw what he meant. Everybody loved good ole Johnny McGrath, but nobody knew why. Ask if they agreed strongly, somewhat, or not at all that he'd be a good man to deal with nuclear disarmament, and you get 70 percent "Agree Strongly." Ask if they agreed strongly, somewhat, or not at all with his plans for nuclear disarmament and there's the same 70 percent again, but this time for "Don't Know."

"You know what?" I said. "Right now Mayor McGrath looks like the perfect vice president—nobody knows enough about him to make him controversial. Just a nice guy for everybody to ignore."

"That's about it. And it's going to be harder for him to turn love into votes in New Hampshire. One other thing I want to show you. There's a tick in the data you ought to watch for. Maybe it doesn't mean a damn thing, but take a look at this." He flipped over half an inch of printouts and rapped the exposed tables with the back of his fingers. "Look here. Three weeks ago, nobody had anything but good to say about this upstanding son of the Middle West. Then week before last four percent flunk him on 'personal integrity.' That got me. Four percent doesn't amount to a thing, and I don't know what personal integrity means, anyway. I just put the damn fool question in on a fishing expedition. So after that turned up, I shoved a couple of extra questions in last week to see if we could get a better handle on what was going on. If anything."

He ran a pencil down the sheet of figures. "So look. This time, seven percent low rating on personal integrity, and when you ask more, it's got nothing to do with behavior in office, but with his private life. Something's making people unhappy, and I haven't been able to find out what. Not yet."

"Seven percent still isn't much," I said, "but I see what you mean. No idea what it's about, huh?"

"None at all. He had a messy divorce about twenty years ago, but hell, so has half the country."

"Messy? How messy?"

"Oh, the usual case of a small town boy getting to be big time and outgrowing his hausfrau. She couldn't take the pressure, started drinking—" He shrugged. "That's all I know about it. It was a page six item in the papers back then, no big deal."

"Doesn't sound like much," I agreed. "Reagan was divorced and it didn't hurt him. There's been worse got itself voted into the White House."

"That's how I figure it, too," Glenn said. "His kids are pretty bad, probably be more trouble than the wife, but I don't think that explains things either."

"How pretty bad?"

"Oh, son George is in his early twenties, and the way I understand it, doesn't do much of anything unless it involves cheap wine, cheap women, and maybe cheap song too. Cracks up the car of the month is how the story goes. Nothing major, but constantly messy, like you wouldn't want to touch him, not without gloves."

"Not good, but that can be handled too."

"If you say so. Eileen, the daughter, is a couple of years older, and from what you hear, whatever it is, she's against it. Makes a pretty decent living as a free-lance journalist, writes articles on women's issues, environmental problems, and she doesn't mind getting in there to pitch some pretty controversial stuff."

"You know, I think I know the name. Isn't she all southern California? Live-in lover of the week, emancipation of the female, picketing something every third Tuesday of the month?"

He nodded. "Like that. She lives in one of those southern California enclaves near L.A. Marina de la Reina. The cocaine shows up every month with the utility bill. At least people think so. You know."

I knew. Marina de la Reina had started out dedicated to the not unreasonable proposition that the young are trendy. Last year they set the mouse traps with brie, but this year brie is for the birds and the mice get goat cheese. Stupid, mildly offensive, but basically harmless. Unfortunately, as is so often the way, the inhabitants soon altered the original premise, as they got older and a shade more desperate, to the assertion that the trendy are young, a dubious proposition that can but lead to age lines and sorrow. Not to mention to a geometrically increasing need to buttress the lie with heavy ingestions of sex, drugs, alcohol, and other substances and activities to which ordinary mortals are rarely privy. A diddle a day keeps the geriatrician away, or something similar. "No particular scandal right now, though, is there?"

"No." He shook his head. "That's another reason I'm puzzled by the polls. Both kids have been quiet lately. It's been a long time since George has piled up a car. Used to be as regular as menstruation. Maybe he's hit menopause. Or maybe they got his license away from him. I hope so, for the candidate's sake."

He fell into silence, but then snapped to and added, "Look, I don't know that any of this means a thing. And as a matter of fact, Al Delaney says the girl at least is a solid citizen underneath the free spirit routine. He even thinks she'll be a help, if it comes to that. And McGrath's mother is a natural too; solid, churchgoing widow lady keeping St. Jo, Missouri in line for the Lord. Well, maybe there's nothing to it, but I figured you'd want to see what I had on this, in case it gets to be important."

"Right. I'll track it in New Hampshire."

"Good. Probably come to nothing, but you never know."

Truer words were never spoke: You never know.

Along about five that afternoon Delaney got hold of Betty, Bill, and me. "We're going to a meeting of the candidates before the debate," he said. "They sit around a table and bullshit about the ground rules, and staff sits around the sides of the room. There's only two rules for us—no talking and no notes. This is strictly a private deal. No reporters get in, no word gets out. Capeesh?"

We capeeshed. Delaney explained that these off-the-record meetings had been initiated because nobody wanted a repeat of what had happened to the Democrats an election or two ago. They had had a large field of candidates scrambling for the nomination, just like now, and it was what you might have expected from a pit crammed with fighting cocks. By the time they had finished savaging each other, the victor had been so thoroughly trashed that old Karl Marx could have beaten him on the Republican ticket, and without getting hardly any blood at all on his beard.

I can't report on any of the substance of the meeting because of the secrecy rule. But some of the byplay I've decided doesn't come under my vow of silence. They had already started when we filed in and quietly took seats at the side. Havemeyer, as the leading candidate, was particularly concerned that nothing occur to jeopardize his position as top dog, and he conducted himself in a way to avoid antagonizing any of the others. "Come on, boys," he was urging as we arrived, "none of us is important, in the final analysis. What matters is that one of us has got to get in, for the good of the country. We can't afford to cut each other up." He smiled beseechingly, but it seemed to me that his humility looked a little smug, the way it is with the richest kid on the block who knows that his shabby jeans were beat up by a big name couturier, and that they are, ultimately, ever so chic, ever so in, and ever so expensive.

Leich, Johnny McGrath's closest competitor, grinned and said, "Yeah, but suppose Johnny here gives me the knee about the space program and starts hooting that there are no separate toilet facilities for women on board ship. Am I supposed to keep quiet?"

Reverend Duckworth jumped in. "Hey, boy, that's my issue. No unisex toilets, even on space ships. That's Godless communism, and you better remember it!" He laughed, but I'd seen warmer smiles on long-gone muskrats by the roadside, their lips drawn back in the rictus of death.

"I defer to the gentleman from Texas," Johnny McGrath said. "How about facilities for the handicapped on board ship? You want that one too, Ducky?"

"Shit, no," Duckworth explained. "Facilities for the handicapped on space ships is a whole different thing, not at all like separate toilet facilities. That's socialist welfare state crap. I'm agin it. Montano gets that one."

"You're too good to me." Montano tapped the table with his fingernails in irritation. "I may take you up on that. Anything I can do to keep the military out of space I'll certainly take under consideration." Montano wasn't big on joking, which turned the party serious.

"You mean you'd like us to be about as well prepared as we were in Vietnam, is that it?" Havemeyer asked, the rich plums in his voice shriveling into prunes. "If you'd been in Saigon at the end, the way I was, you wouldn't be so damn sure that confining the military to crossbows and broad swords was necessarily the best thing for the country."

"Oh, can it, Dick," McGrath put in crossly. "We're not going after you in public on that Vietnam bull of yours, we agreed to that, but right here in this room we all know that if you were in Saigon at the end it was because you were still typing up a letter the general wanted to get out that day. So cool it, at least with us, okay?"

Again there was laughter. I saw the need for these meetings. These characters were standing in a circle with guns to each other's heads, and if they all pulled the triggers at once, well, it'd be back to the old drawing board, election-wise.

"Hey, Ducky," Leich inquired, "if you're so devoted to the pious folk who made America great and not to the big moneybags, how come that rock on your little finger? How do you explain that?"

"Which rock on which little finger?" Duckworth asked innocently.

"Offhand," Havemeyer suggested, "I'd say the man meant the diamond rock on your left pinky, the one set in eighteen carat gold and resting so comfortably on your belly, reverend."

"Oh, *that* rock! That's not a diamond. It's a love stone, given to me by the tens of thousands of dear souls who have benefited from my ministry." He smiled, daring anyone to contradict.

"Is that what it is? You could've fooled me," McGrath admitted. "Tell me, who do you have to kiss to get a love stone like that?"

"In my case, nobody," Duckworth answered, "but for the rest of you, it isn't so much who you kiss—bankers, farmers, labor bosses, anybody—as where you kiss 'em. Right, Dick?" he asked Havemeyer, who had been getting himself a reputation for promising anything to anyone who could deliver the votes. Not that the others objected to the principle, but they were jealous of the way Havemeyer made it work without ever getting himself backed into a corner by all those promises.

"I'm glad it's only the God of Love you preach," Havemeyer rejoined, his face turning an ugly red. "I'd hate to be around when you hook up with a more vengeful deity, Ducky, And I'm sure you will, some day, no matter what name you call him by."

"Now, Dick," McGrath reproved, "take it easy on old Vern. Let's not lose our cool. I thought these get-togethers were supposed to help us push these personal attacks out of the way. Anyway, you know damn well Vern isn't going to switch deities, not with all those good born-again folk standing behind him. Much more likely he'll work on getting them two votes apiece, one for each birth."

Montano found this funny, and his guffaw sounded like a bicycle tire popping. Duckworth shot him a vicious look, as if marking him for celestial retribution at some later date.

And so it went. The boys were just not overly fond of each other. I didn't know how they were going to keep it from showing in public, but they were the political experts, not me. I suppose it was like the crooked cops in a TV show: They were out to beat the hell out of each other as nastily as possible, but without leaving any marks that could be held against them later, especially if the other guy should win the day.

☐ FIVE ☐

It was the eve of the second debate. The candidates were to sit in the audience, mount the platform individually for brief opening statements, and return to their auditorium seats. Following that, they were to march on together and sit behind a table facing the audience. A moderator, profile to the house, was to position himself at the end of the table. The rules had been concocted that way because seven of the candidates had complained about the Reverend Duckworth upstaging their opening remarks at the first debate. He had been accused of holding private conferences with the Heavenly Being, he and his good buddy in the sky dancing a mad fandango, the reverend naturally taking the lead, while the other candidates flapped about like headless chickens, trying to get a modicum of attention from the audience.

The first row of the auditorium was reserved for the candidates. Staff and the press were in the next few rows, where Betty and I sat flanking Al Delaney. I noticed my companions' knees touching a couple of times through, I must charitably assume, inadvertence. Where Bill Toscani was I had no idea, though I imagined he was somewhere around if he hadn't accidentally got himself locked in a booth in the men's room.

The moment arrived. The candidates entered through a door next to the stage and headed for their seats. There was a polite scattering of applause. Music, or an approximation thereof, filled the air with a startling suddenness. Heads swiveled toward the balcony, and there, conveniently centered in the first row for the television cameras, was a gaggle of Duckworth supporters singing "The Eyes of Texas Are upon You," accompanied by finger cymbals, kazoos, ocarinas, and a piccolo, instruments small enough to smuggle past the security guards at the entry.

Duckworth himself mugged a form of happy surprise that telegraphed the information that he wasn't really surprised at all, and wasn't he the clever puss to pretend to it and still let everybody in on his naughty secret. "That bastard," Delaney snorted. "Listen, if the eyes of Texas are upon Duckworth, Texas is gazing up its own asshole. Shit!" He emphasized the expletive by bringing a hand down firmly on Betty's thigh, a good politician never losing his feel for the priorities.

The hall quieted down. Montano was the first candidate to mount the platform, the order of speaking having been determined by drawing lots. He frankly stated his position as a one issue candidate, the issue being nuclear disarmament. He asked for votes even if the voter didn't think he could win. It wouldn't be a vote thrown away because with sufficient backing he could force the winner to pay attention to this life or death problem. The applause was respectable but unenthusiastic, like that accorded a high school senior at graduation for four years of straight A's for conduct. I looked around. People were sitting on their hands, and would probably remain that way until Des Moines was glowing in the dark. One young woman two rows back wasn't even looking at the stage, and judging from her blank expression and plunging neckline I wondered if she had perhaps arrived a few hours before the next scheduled event, maybe try-outs for an X-rated movie. As a matter of fact, my eye lingered a while because the woman's face was somewhere between striking and zany, with light brown hair too carefully dyed, wide gray eyes too heavily lashed, and a mouth that was almost certainly sufficiently lush even without the slathering of lipstick that covered it. There was a disturbingly inappropriate air to her, as if I had run into a model from a TV cosmetics commercial squeezing melons in a supermarket.

Havemeyer was up next. He opened his mouth and the Winds of Praise for Democracy blew flatulently around the hall, anesthetizing all in their path. He briefly proclaimed his independence of all groups that were supporting him—labor, farmers, senior citizens, minorities—and then equally briefly proclaimed his support for all those groups he was independent of—labor, farmers, senior citizens, minorities. And of course the middle class, just in case anybody felt left out. He got a livelier reception, possibly because nobody could figure out what he was saying, so nobody was put off by it. And somebody there had to be a laborer, farmer, senior citizen, minority. Or else a member of the great middle class.

McGrath headed up next while I was still looking around to judge the applause. The strange young lady's blank face had taken on a more agitated look, and while I was focusing more or less in her direction, she suddenly got to her feet and pointed what looked alarmingly like a revolver, toy-type. It happened so fast I couldn't be sure, but the way I saw it, she wasn't set to bang away at Johnny or at anybody else, but up in the air over the stage, as if she were trying to goose the bare-ass plaster angels that were hanging onto the proscenium arch by their fingernails.

She was yelling, but so were three dozen other members of the audience, so there was no way to know what she was yelling about. A nearby citizen sprang up and slammed the gun out of her hand. A crew of plainclothesmen was all over Johnny, squashing him to the floor and out of harm's way. The general public was either charging one way and another or else frozen statue-still.

TV cameras were grinding. The crowd was shrieking. Johnny was hustled offstage and Al Delaney damn near shoved me through the back of my seat in his push to reach his man. A voice, the moderator's, I think, called through a microphone for calm, but I doubt that many people could have heard him, and few of those paid any heed. A crew of uniformed men pushed down an aisle jammed with people struggling to get out, as if a smoking gun, even though removed from the villain's grasp, constituted a form of contagion. The guards reached the would-be assassin and grabbed her as they would have grabbed a temporarily motionless panther, which indeed she might have been. They rushed her off with her feet scarcely touching the floor, the crowd parting in advance of them magically, like the Red Sea for the children of Israel. I watched the faces of the crowd as the woman was hustled out, and they ran a couple of gamuts: There were those who looked directly at her, their expressions ranging from fear to anger to hatred, while others looked away, either to avoid the evil eye or because their mothers had taught them that staring was impolite. At another extreme I actually spotted two lowlifes helpless in their seats with knee-slapping mirth. It takes all kinds, they say, but I can't see why.

It was the best miniseries on TV for the next two days, much more fun for the viewing audience than for those who were on the scene. Vernon Duckworth had grabbed more camera time than would have seemed humanly possible, considering that it wasn't his show. There were shots of the man on his knees, palms together in front of his chest (diamond pinky ring glistening passionately), looking upward in prayer. There were shots of him on his feet, arms extended in prayer. There were no shots of him standing on his hands and looking downward to excoriate the devil, but I'm positive there would have been if he had had the time to go out for a course in gymnastics. By the time the babble had subsided sufficiently for any particular noises to dominate, Duckworth was front and center to lead his balcony brigade in a splendid rendition of "Shall We Gather at the River." If there was a winner that day, outside of the TV advertisers, it was good old Vern, who knew more about show biz than most of the directors in Hollywood.

Oh, yes, the would-be murderess. She was present, too, and ultimately the newscasters dropped, with obvious reluctance, their earnest commentary on Duckworth's bravery, and got around to her. Not too much of her, because after she was hustled off they could only talk about her, for heaven's sake, and the definition of news these days is whatever you can get a good camera angle on. Anything else is for eggheads or funny old-fashioned things like newspapers.

Della DeGraaf was her name, or at least that was what she had been christened by her agent when she had her brief and forgettable career as a child actress in TV commercials and lesser movies. Della was the one who disappeared into the maw of the evil parsnip from the planet Argola in the first reel. When she wasn't doing that, she was on TV ingesting bowls of whatever cereal contained minimum daily requirements of one thing or another recently discovered by some conglomerate's pet biologists. She had dropped from view a few years before, due to a nervous and absent-minded predilection for sopping up liquid from round bottles more avidly than the square-boxed riboflavin and fiber she was being paid to shovel down.

Della had, we were informed, been hooting that Johnny McGrath had promised to marry her, and she had come all the way from California to force him to redeem his promise. She had added to that the strong suggestion that she was large with the man's very own unborn child. Johnny was quoted as saying he had never known her, in either the biblical or popular sense, and a team of doctors observed that if she was large with anything at all it was alcohol-related fatty tissue. The question of whose unborn what she was or wasn't large with was irrelevant—except to the voters, who checked in with a 13 percent disapproval of the candidate on the personal integrity ladder in Glenn's next day survey.

There were two other peculiar, if less sensational, items. The gun had been stolen several weeks earlier in Boston, a fact no one could make sense of, so naturally forgot. And I thought I had seen the lady aim up in the air, but everybody figured I was wrong and they forgot about that, too. So did I.

A sizable share of the folk who had been McGrath supporters but were now voicing their moral disapproval switched their preference to Duckworth, according to the survey. That was a matter for some discussion. "I don't know," Al Delaney said, "but even if it was a setup, I still don't make it Vernon Duckworth. Not his style."

"I agree," McGrath said. "Vernon's too shrewd for anything that clumsy. And you've got to admit he's got some standards. I suppose it could have been one of the freaks supporting him, but we'll never know." He sighed. "With luck, we'll never need to know, either."

But life isn't all that simple. Once some screwball starts a pattern, great gaggles turn up in short order to play follow the leader. And so two days later it was open season on candidates again. Betty, Al, Bill, and I were waiting in the hotel lobby for McGrath to join us in a breakfast strategy meeting where we were to bounce ideas off each other and the rubberized scrambled eggs for containing this small nonexistent scandal before it could burgeon into a large nonexistent scandal. Daughter Eileen, who had flown in to be with her father, was coming along as well.

The McGraths were late. We had run out of conversation and were slumped quietly, each of us accommodating his or her frame to the vagaries of the erratically sprung uneasy chairs. The other livestock in the lobby, men waiting for their wives so they could get on the road, kids waiting for their parents so they could eat, and the staring lost ones who people every hotel lobby in the world waiting without a clear sense of what they may be waiting for—love, sex, insight, even a decent burial—all sat with varying degrees of patience or restlessness.

The candidate finally arrived, daughter Eileen on his arm. The impatience must have shown on our faces. "Sorry," the man explained, "but it's Eileen's fault. Couldn't get her clothes on straight. Says it's the middle of the night back home." I looked at the daughter, whom I was seeing for the first time, and didn't know whether to be relieved or disappointed. I think I was unconsciously anticipating an Amazon either swaddled in a sari and sandals or sporting a topless vinyl outfit with black leather boots, a leashed ocelot in one hand and a similarly leashed lover in the other. What I got was a young brunette with a firm chin and blue eyes that looked capable of incinerating an enemy tank at fifty yards, between blinks. Her clothes rated a stare, all right, but only for elegance, not for being far out.

The night before, after her arrival, she and daddy, together with Betty and Al, had gone to the city's leading private club for dinner. Betty told me later that when the maître d' murmured his regrets that ladies in trousers could not be seated for the evening meal, Eileen smiled, said, "They can be now," and swept in without missing a beat. And when one of the hosts said he hoped her father was in favor of denying unfriendly countries access to good American wheat, she asked sweetly if he'd prefer to start by starving kids in Africa or dictators in South America.

And here she was, trim, tough, and tasty. She replied to her father by saying, "That's a sexist position, Dad, blaming the woman for not being ready on time. And there goes the feminist vote."

"Including yours?" Johnny asked.

"I haven't made up my mind as yet."

"That's a very female thing, too," Johnny riposted.

We all laughed discreetly, which got us stared at by the other folks in the lobby. Some stared because they recognized the candidate, I imagine, and others only because the sound of a warm human voice is so unlikely in the shoddy purgatories that masquerade as entry lounges in most hotels. One squatter went so far as to rise from his seat and point. A revolver. "The devil hath many faces," a strangely high voice informed us, but whether he was referring to his own countenance or one of ours was never made clear before the shrieking started. The gun went off; the candidate dropped. The gun went off again, and it spun Betty Gold's shoulder bag into half a loop. That marvelous woman, quicker on the uptake than the rest, followed through on the spin and clobbered the assailant, by now only a few feet away and coming on fast. She caught him across the face, knocking a pair of steel-rimmed glasses into a skid across the lobby floor.

Bill, Al, Eileen, and I lunged, doing as much damage to each other as to the gunman, but we got him down, his skull crunching pleasantly on the marble chip flooring. "You bastard!" Eileen screamed, the words sandpapered as they were torn out of her throat.

She ran back to her father, who was holding his arm and

struggling to sit up, his face contorted. The rest of us kept our boy flat on the floor while Betty yelled to the desk clerk, who had been stunned into rigidity, to get a doctor and call the police.

Our sword of the Lord editorialized loudly. "Whore of Babylon!" he shouted in Eileen McGrath's direction, lifting his bloody head off the floor to do so. "The sins of the father—"

He stopped right there because Al Delaney, hands trembling, swatted him back and forth across the face twice before I grabbed his arm. "Cool it," I snapped. "The guy's hurt. That won't help." The guy's nose was bleeding now. "Go help Eileen with Johnny. I'll sit on this one myself."

There was, for once, a doctor in the house, and he came forward to reveal himself without any apparent fear of malpractice suits. He got working on Johnny's arm, and after announcing that it didn't look bad, sterilized and bandaged it temporarily with supplies from the hotel's emergency kit. Then he disappeared, perhaps concerned about lawsuits after all.

The cops and medics arrived in short order and variously removed Johnny to a hospital and the divinely appointed nut to the pokey, though not before the latter, courage increasing proportionately to the number of cops between himself and everybody else, howled, "'Vengeance is mine, saith the Lord!' Yeah, and—" Al Delaney rushed at him, police or no police, and the sermon took on a more practical tone: "Stop him! He's crazy!"

"He should know what crazy is, that bastard," Betty muttered.

The man turned out to be an unemployed auto worker who blamed his woes on godless Japanese and by extension on anyone else who fell beyond his own special definition of godliness. He was one of the kooks who travel in the wake of political campaigns like gulls around the garbage behind a ship at sea. And Duckworth was his candidate of choice. The rest of his story, taken down to its zany essentials, was that he disapproved of daughter Eileen's liberated views and had concluded, somehow, that the sins of the daughter ought to be visited on the father, which may well make as much sense as the other way around.

McGrath's arm was in a sling, his right arm. Which got him off the handshaking circuit for a while, though he occasionally gripped a potential voter's fingers with his left hand, a gesture judged as especially sincere by the fingers' owners. The other candidates one and all clucked and deplored, greatly and at length. Except for that old shrewdy Vernon Duckworth, who asked forgiveness for the sinner, leaving unclear whether that designation covered the gunman, McGrath, or both, and followed through on this request with a prayer that the Lord might spare His servant John McGrath and return him to good health. The Lord cooperated, this requiring very little effort on His part, and among the right set Ducky got the equivalent of three or four touchdowns. Johnny got perhaps a touchdown's worth of sympathy, minus a fraction because of the where-there's-smoke-there's-fire syndrome, for a net gain of maybe one field goal. And the director of the local hospital got lots of free television coverage, but he didn't have a personality that projected well at all, so I doubt that it helped his practice.

Al Delaney dismissed the incident's potential for affecting the campaign. "Hell," he said, "it's not like with the DeGraaf clown. The Duckworth people are loaded with freaks and everybody knows it. They figure they're too good to need redemption themselves, and they'd be too mean to accept it if it came their way anyway. So they look for somebody else to lay it on. You know what I mean: 'You'll behave if I have to kill you to make you do it.' Like that. And I'd stake my next ten beers Duckworth himself had nothing to do with it."

He dismissed the matter with a wave of the hand. "Nobody's gonna take them seriously," he reassured us, "people like that. Like with the Montano crowd at the other end, the ones who eat up guilt like it's an ice cream sundae and blame themselves for every defective brake that kills a kid and for every baby that dies of malnutrition in Africa. The voters don't buy that either."

It looked like he was right. The candidates charged about like computer-programmed mechanical toys. Leich came out for gun control, which did him no good. Havemeyer, still all things to all men, women, and hermaphrodites, and furthermore not wanting to offend the National Rifle Association or the gun control advocates, opted to call for a renascence of public morality. Big deal. Montano, by way of some strangely contorted logic, found the incident to be proof positive of the need for unilateral disarmament, which did nothing for him either.

Everything was grist for everybody's mill, and all those little mills were grinding out, they each fervently prayed, lots of votes.

I came out for getting my nerve-shattered carcass away from the gun-toting frontier lands and back to the bucolic pastures of midtown Manhattan. Maybe you can get shot down in New York the same way as in Iowa, but they do it without a lengthy libretto to explain the action. They just *do* it. Quietly, like reasonable, dignified killers.

❑
SIX
❑

I got my wish for a return to Manhattan, but I got it hung on me like in one of those sadistic fairy tales where the old sow of a witch grants your wishes but makes them all turn sour.

Back at the hotel that evening I found a message to call Ed Jorgensen any time I got in, day or night. I got him at his home in Connecticut and he summoned me home for an urgent meeting in the morning, which meant finding some sort of transportation out of Des Moines that night. *That night!* I checked the airport and got myself booked on a 2:30 A.M. flight, which, as I've already said, didn't get off the ground until dawn. (For only the fourteenth time that day I mooned listlessly about early retirement on an apple orchard about eighty miles or so north of New York City, an apple orchard where ad agency presidents would be sprayed as ruthlessly as tent caterpillars, apple scab, and apple borers. More ruthlessly perhaps; caterpillars, scab, and borers don't make noise.)

Before I left I had a session with Al Delaney in the hotel bar to talk over my plans for the polling in New Hampshire. "The kids who're working for Johnny," he explained, "will be your interviewers. College students, mostly. All you've got to do is tell 'em what questions to ask. And we got one terrific break, praise be. One of these computer whiz kids who runs his own shop outside Boston is with us, and he's put in a system in Manchester so you can do your interviews right on the computer, whatever the hell that means. You know what I'm talking about? Because I'm not sure I know what I'm talking about myself."

"That's great. Two things—what's the guy's name, and do you know if he's got a random dialing arrangement?"

"I don't know from random dialing," Delaney replied. "But he's got everything else, so why not random dialing? Anyway, you'll have to check it out for yourself. His name is Daitch. Josh Daitch. He and his old lady Ginny, they own the joint. Together they add up to twenty years old, it looks to me, like all computer types, and they've been running this Route 128 place, Numbers Unlimited, for five years anyway, so you figure it out. Me, it depresses. You figure," he repeated, "and when you do, don't tell me about it."

"My pleasure. Look, I've got my plane to New York coming up, so why don't we get down to cases. Let's get Betty and Bill down here and talk about what happens next."

We did that, and by the time it was over Betty and Bill had started sketching out plans for handbills, radio and TV spots, print ads, and special events.

Delaney nodded his satisfaction. "Good. The three of you have a pretty good feel by now for what we're trying to get across. Just let me give you a couple of tips to keep in mind when you're working up this stuff. There are three rules for public office candidates in this country that can't be violated," he said, waggling a finger unevenly, "and it can't even look like Johnny's even vaguely thinking about violating them. You get me?"

I got him, and I also got the idea his drinks were doing the talking. "Not yet," I said, "but try us."

He rattled the ice and belted down the dregs. "First, a candidate can never insult the flag or question the valor of our fighting men, even indirectly. Generals excepted. Generals are fair game. Likewise admirals. They're fat and they're old, which every good American hates automatically. Second, no candidate can admit to having had sex, or even to having thought about it in his heart, except as a patriotic duty to procreate, and even that'd be better if you could put it out that he found his kids under cabbage leaves. And third, no candidate should ever, under any circumstances, no matter what, sodomize a mule unless the mule promises to keep its mouth shut. You got that?"

I put my glass down hard. "I think it must be later than I think it is, and I've got to get going. Maybe I'll stick in a question like, 'Which candidate do most mules in this town go for? Why is that?'" I turned to my coworkers. "Either of you two headed back tonight?"

"Lord, no!" Toscani said. He grinned. "Jorgensen's riding your tail about something, huh? Flying all night, for God's sake!"

Betty said nothing. Delaney spoke up for her. "Betty here is staying on a couple of days. If she's going to set Johnny up for inspecting ski lifts and pitching hay back East, I want her to get to know his style a little better."

I raised an eyebrow. "Get a feel for the lay of the land, you mean? Something like that?"

"Something like that," Delaney said modestly, while Betty guffawed and gave me a playful punch. Since she was a lady who still thought thin even though several stone past that condition, it hurt.

Bill and I took the elevator up together. "Do you think there's something going on with those two? I get this feeling."

"Betty and Al?" I asked in surprise. "That's the last thing I'd be thinking." And the next to the last, and the thing before that as well, but why disillusion anything as sweet and innocent as an account executive?

SEVEN

Sally looked up from her typewriter when I walked in midmorning, unfresh from the airport, red-eyed, bearded, and sullen. "Hail, the king-maker," she lied. "All hail. How'd it go?"

"Well, *I* haven't made any kings in the last couple of days; how about you? Doin' all right?"

"I was till now." She cut the banter. "No fooling, Ev, how'd it go?"

"Okay, I guess, but I'm too beat to talk about it now. Would you get me a cup of coffee, Sal? I need it bad. And would you ask Jane to come in?"

She considered my request according to the rules promulgated by the women's movement, and then, nothing if not fair, announced, "Right. I'll get you your coffee. I figure you'd ask even a male secretary to do it when you're tired like this, so it's not a sexist demand. Not," she added firmly, "this time." She went out.

Jane came in and pecked me on the cheek. "You look awful," she stated cheerfully. "Too many dusky native girls out there?"

I thought of Della DeGraaf. "Something like that. I'll tell you about them tonight." We had a rule, Jane and I, that we talked personal matters at home, up in the East Eighties, and kept office business confined to midtown, to be shot dead if it were seen trying to cross north of Fifty-ninth Street.

"Okay, dear, you just take it easy today." Jane knew what business travel did to me: The inside of my head invariably ended up like the inside of my suitcase—messy, slightly soiled, and impossible to locate anything in. Nature intended me to live a quiet life in the Hudson Valley, where I grew up, far from Madison Avenue, and to be master, along with Jane and Billy, Jane's son from her first marriage, of the apple orchard. Depending on the season I could always see the orchard in my mind's eye filled with pink blossoms, green leaves, red globes, or bare brown branches outlined with a snow whose whiteness was not grimed over by soot and grease after two days, the way it is in the city.

"Thanks," I said. "Everything normal here, then, whatever that may be?"

"Just about. We had a crew working most of two nights to get the cigarette name test ready for the client meeting, and we made it fine. Time to spare, even." Our tobacco client was launching a new menthol cigarette, and we had a survey under way to find out which of a set of possibilities for the brand name had the most market appeal.

"What came in first?"

"Almost a tie. Green Lites and City Lites. Either one would work. Green Lites is a little better with older smokers who think menthol butts are easier on the throat.

City Lites worked best with the kids who, you know, still have the idea that puffing away makes them all elegance and sophistication."

"I hope they stay away from City Lites, then. I hate trying to rope kids into smoking. Which one did the client pick?"

"You get your wish. They decided against City Lites."

"Good."

"And against Green Lites, too. They're going to call it Green Glows." Jane's voice was grim.

"So why? What the hell's that all about!"

"And it came in near the bottom. People said Green Glows sound like fire, like it'd burn their throats. Sounded hot, they said."

"Come on, Jane, let me have it. Why?"

"The usual. Their chief executive officer's daughter thought it up, that's why. She's eighteen and lusting after a career in advertising, glamour division, first class."

"Why didn't the goddamn account man squash it?"

"Squash it! Oh, Ev, you know what account men are like. He said it was great, the shit."

I knew what account men are like, all right. Anything to keep the client happy, even if it works against his product's long term advantage. By the time it bombs, the account man will have moved on to a more glorious job at a bigger agency. Not the really smart account execs, of course, but most of them. In fact, for the most part the very notion of a smart account exec is a contradiction in terms, like pygmy basketball players or poverty stricken brain surgeons.

Don't get the idea that I'm bitter; there's no stauncher defender of account men than me. At some time or other a rumor was deliberately circulated that account executives were shepherded each morning by their wives to the various commuter train stations that ring New York City like hostile Indian encampments, and that upon arrival in the parking lots the wives would slap labels reading THIS END up on the family breadwinners' teensy brows before pointing them toward the 8:15. Because of the many millions jealous of the poor fellows for their beauty, chic, bank accounts, and ability to transmogrify gracefully into quivering lumps of craven-flavor jelly at the approach of a frowning client, the vile calumny gained wide and effective currency.

I did my best to stop it, pointing out that the story was as untrue as it was vicious. First, the wives are invariably too busy with their own affairs for such luxurious courtesies, whether these include ferrying youngsters to schools in station wagons, nursing hangovers, or arranging clandestine trysts with tennis pros in country club boathouses. Furthermore, even without the labels, most of the hapless hubbies could be relied on to reach Manhattan without mishap, right side up, each and every weekday morning.

I grant you a certain percentage would invariably disembark at Larchmont or 125th Street under the impression that they had reached Grand Central Station, but that's a totally different story, and not at all what I'm talking about right now.

All this, plus the expedition to Des Moines and I was less than my usual ebullient self. "Screw them all. I hope the brand goes under, sinks without a trace." My gang had worked two nights in a row on that name test because it was what is laughingly called urgent. And now the only urgency was to get the results into the trash bin in time for the morning pickup. "Did you tell the kids about it?"

"Not me, buster. You're the boss. You tell 'em."

Jane was right. Whether I liked it or not, psychiatric guidance is the major part of a boss's job. I asked Joe Harris to join us. Joe had been head of the crew that had labored heroically those two nights, and he sagged when I told him, omitting only the role of the eighteen-year-old genius who had chosen the brand name, that his findings had been dismissed. "I'm sorry, Joe, I really am. But look at it this way: You did your best, and if the product's any good it'll make it anyway, and if it doesn't, the fault won't be yours. There might even be some pleasure in watching it sink. You did your job, so the devil with them. Anyway, what does it matter? You remember the Buick thing?"

He nodded and brightened slightly, the sun making the vaguest of shadows as the storm clouds began to clear away. I was talking about a classic bit of insanity back when cigarettes were still allowed to advertise on television. There's a dilemma in TV advertising: If a commercial gives the important facts about a product, seriously and honestly, the audience won't pay any attention; they want to be amused, not educated. But if a commercial is highly entertaining, viewers will burble like infants at the fun and not catch the facts, sometimes not even the name of the brand. One day came the lovely moment when there were two entertaining commercials being run during the same season, and for some mystic reason buried deep within the national psyche, the public muddled them together in a sort of mental food processor. When advertising researchers asked what the message was, a glorious proportion joyfully trilled—

"Wouldn't you really rather have a Byoooo-ICK
Than a-
Ny o-
Ther Fil-
Ter cig-
ARETTE!"

Joe seemed mollified, at least a little, and I didn't have to dip into the reserves, including—

"I wonder
Where the
Yellow

>   Went on
>   Tyrone
>   Power's
>   Teeth."

After the poor fellow left my office I called Jorgensen to report in and ask why I was needed back in New York so urgently. His secretary answered. "Oh, gee, I'm sorry, honey, but he took off for the Coast this morning. He said he'd see you when he got back."

Milquetoast that I am, I did not reply, "Not if I can help it, he won't." Instead, I asked, "Do you know what it's about?"

"No, I'm afraid I don't. I guess it'll keep or he would have said something."

"Thanks, anyway."

I looked at my watch. It was getting on toward noon of a rainy Monday morning. The foul weather had followed me east from Iowa. I wondered if Big Ed had peremptorily summoned it to New York the way he had me. I got up, hefted the office umbrella and walked out. "Bye-bye, Sally," I said. "See you tomorrow."

Once home I headed straight for the bed, pausing only to set the alarm for 2:30. That wouldn't catch me up completely on my sleep, but it'd get me looking approximately alive when Billy got home from school. Somewhere within me rests the foolish notion that if a kid sees a parent, even a stepparent, in bed during daylight hours, it destroys his moral fiber and leads but to the analyst's couch. No need to tell me it's idiotic; Billy did that himself. "Hi, Ev," he said, seconds after dumping his books, "you look icky. Why don't you go to bed or something?"

Defeated, I did. We should all listen to our betters. Jane got in at six and served up cocktails in bed, which is really living, and which is also as much debauchery as this old frame can cope with these days. She and Billy joined me, one sitting on each side. "Don't jiggle, you two," I warned. "I'd rather have the coroner find the gin on the inside, if it's all the same to you."

Billy responded by balancing a bowl of peanuts on my stomach. "How's about peanuts in the belly button?" he inquired politely.

"With or without lint?" I asked. "Ya gotta be specific, kid."

Jane was impatient. "All right, you two, cut the comedy. I want to know what went on out there. The news has been full of it. What are those guys like, anyway?"

"What are they like? I don't know what to say. Like everybody else who thinks he's important. A bunch of turkeys masquerading as peacocks and hoping they can get a lot of other people to believe it. They just want to be president is the main thing different about them."

"Any of them good enough?"

I looked helpless. "I don't know. What's good enough? All of these guys have the idea that maybe if you can't fool all the people all the time, maybe at least you can fool enough of the people enough of the time to get away with it.

"Havemeyer is going to get the nomination, and he's as good as any of them, even if he would promise his grandmother's scalp to the Indians to get himself Oklahoma. And if you ask me, our boy McGrath is just as acceptable, for whatever that's worth. Anything you've heard about Duckworth is unfortunately true, but unless the country is but really off its rocker he won't make it." I paused. "I guess in their own ways they all occasionally mean well, which is the most I can say for them."

"Sounds dismal."

"Yeah, yeah," Billy said impatiently, "that's okay, but what about all that shooting, huh?"

"Yeah," echoed my equally bloodthirsty wife, "what about that?"

"What can I tell you? There've been nuts taking pot shots at politicians for a century and a half. Dangerous cranks, which is bad enough, but with luck, this'll be the end to it, at least for this election."

"Is that all you've got to say?" Jane asked. Billy looked bored. "A little ninth-rate philosophy is all?"

"You know as much about it as I do if you caught it on the news. A couple of idiots waving guns around, and if they don't understand it themselves, how the hell can I? Yes, that's all I've got to say." I suppose I sounded like an irritated old lady, but I'd had enough of that Des Moines business. I changed the subject. "What do I have to do to get something to eat around here?" I demanded.

"Get out of bed and get dressed," Jane suggested.

"And wash your hands," Billy ordered.

"That depends," I countered, "on what's to eat."

"We call it chicken dinner à la campaign trail. Quartered fryers deep-fried in properly aged lukewarm oil."

"And," Billy added eagerly, "soft french fries that won't hurt your ole teeth. I made them myself before I went to school. Yesterday."

I got up anyway. After all, the next day was Tuesday, which wouldn't be so bad, since I had had a small break from sitting in my Finch, Rowan, & Hyde torture chamber, and after Tuesday came sacred Wednesday. I've never been a Thank God It's Friday believer, though I've pretended to it so I wouldn't look insane to my coworkers. For me Wednesday's always been the one to hold out for. Monday and Tuesday are uphill, and so is Wednesday morning. But then, 1:00 P.M. on Wednesday, lovely, 1:00 P.M., half the work week is over and the downhill stretch gets underway. Twenty hours behind you and twenty hours up front; twenty-one in the rear, nineteen ahead; twenty-two done with, eighteen to go; twenty-three . . . peace, it's wonderful.

EIGHT

For those of us with sufficient good taste to be over thirty, there are only three seasons in New Hampshire: spring (what there is of it), summer, and fall. Winter is a judgment. Yet here I was in Manchester in February. The frost was on the pumpkin, and the pumpkin was the end of my nose.

With nobody around I could legitimately hate, I focused on the motel, a dispirited edifice thrown up *(sic)* in an era when motels were designed to express their personalities by way of nile green tiled fountains, possibly powered by swamp gas, in their lobbies, like the heads on pimples. Most specimens have small coins sulking amid the algae in the murkey depths, but mine was less luxurious; it was instead festooned with pre-chewed bubble gum, wrappers included.

Such is life on the campaign trail, and complaint is pointless. Primaries are a major industry, and every hotel, motel, and rooming house in Manchester—New Hampshire's chief entry in the big city league—was overloaded with candidates and their families, paid staff, volunteers, hired extras (like me), and the hangers-on along for whatever glamour or excitement they could persuade themselves they were experiencing. Beyond that were the subsidiary low-life industries like gamblers making book, call girls making delegates, and reporters making stories. Local services were beefed up, including souvenir shops, laundries, restaurants, and an assortment of roadhouses, bars, and nightclubs, more than one of which tacked up notices boasting that they could offer the greatest little combo now appearing anywhere in the East between Lewiston, Maine and White River Junction, Vermont.

"The LeGrand bunch are quoting three to one or better against Johnny for win, place, or show," Delaney informed me grimly. "They've even got him fourth or fifth, behind Havemeyer, Leich, Duckworth, and, God help us, maybe Montano, too."

"What's the LeGrand bunch?" I asked. "Local pollsters? Never heard of 'em."

He looked disgusted. "Come on, now, man. Pierre LeGrand. The syndicate man for this part of the world, everybody says. French Canadian. Bookies, girls, drugs, you name it. When the LeGrand crowd sets the odds, they got their reasons, damn it."

"Oh," I said brightly. "I get it. I guess you don't need me then, pal. Get Monseer LeGrand to look at some chicken entrails and tell you what's up. I can get back to New York. Okay?"

"So it's dumb. I know it. I'm not saying they're right, but it's something to think about, LeGrand putting our boy in the cellar. Like I say, they do that, they've got their reasons."

"Fine. You think about it. Me, I'll do what you're paying me for, and that goes for Toscani and Gold, too. Or should we send Betty home, you think? Waste of money to have her here?"

He grinned and even looked foolish, which he had every right to look. "You've noticed. No, leave her here. And you two guys can stick around too."

"Too generous," I murmured modestly.

"Okay, okay. Enough. You win. I'm a jerk. Don't rub it in. Let's get on with it, huh? You've gone over what we want you to cover in the polls?"

I nodded. "It's all laid out for the interviewers."

"Good. I'll take a look later. Let's go see how the whiz kids are set up now." He took me by the arm and led the way down a flight of stairs from the motel lobby. "Here we are, pal," he said, steering me around a bend to the double doors of a meeting room. In harmony with the generally modish ambience of the establishment, the sign alongside the doors read, "Lizard Lounge."

Inside there were tables lining three walls, and a desk on the fourth, a short wall with a view over the rest of the room. The tables were topped with computer terminals and viewing screens for maybe a dozen interviewers. A young couple stood up from a huddle over one of the units and ambled easily toward us. "Hey," the male said, "I'm Josh Daitch, and this is Ginny. You must be Ev Franklin. Good to have you here. We've been looking forward to meeting you."

I saw what Delaney meant about computer kids, and why it depressed him. The Daitches were near look-alikes, with skin stretched tight and fleshless over fine bones, clear eyes (brown for him, blue for her), light brown hair (for both) that tumbled over foreheads, and long and slender frames. They radiated jogging suits, yogurt, tofu, and whole-grain comestibles without preservatives. They were, at first glance, eternal twenty-fives. At second glance, they were tired twenty-fives, and if you were so jealously uncharitable as to peer at them yet again, they were youthful miracles of thirty-five. They flashed smiles of health and beauty through the kind of teeth that drive real people hysterical with longing.

"Good to be here. This looks great," I said, waving a hand at the arrangements and at a group of youngsters babbling happily around the front desk.

"Don't mind them," Daitch said. "They're your interviewers, and they're panting to get started. Hey, you over there!" he called. "Come meet the boss!"

The healthiest group of apple-cheeked babes I had ever seen outside a cereal commercial (where they're largely over-pancaked midgets, if you ask me) crossed the room, all eagerness and curiosity. Having spent my adult life in the big city, I had to squelch an impulse to assume that any outstretched youthful hands headed toward me were aimed at my wallet, my gullet, or both.

"Hi," I said, "greetings. If you're all as eager as you look, and if this setup here is as good as it looks—and I'm sure you are and it is—then I'll only say I'm delighted to be here, and I don't see any reason we can't get right to it and start putting our man over the top." (Call me scoutmaster, first class.) "I've got the first questionnaire right here with me, and while there may be a few changes after Mr. Delaney has gone over it, we can look at it together and I'll answer any questions. Unless they're too tough." There was an appreciative laugh at the old gentleman's mock modesty. "If somebody'll help me pass these out we're in business."

An excited, happy hum buzzed around the room. Faced with all that bounce and buoyance I felt like Dorian Gray thirty years after the lad had first started mucking about in the fog-shrouded sinks of London's East End.

I should explain a little something about computerized interviewing. These days, control of surveys has reached a point where it's getting harder for interviewers to make mistakes, ask the wrong questions or leave some questions out, whether by accident or by design. And it's even getting less likely that they'll interview the wrong person or the wrong household. With a system like the one we had here, the interviewers don't make the phone calls; the computer picks the numbers and even dials them. A survey company will find out what telephone exchanges are used for residential phones and how many phones there are on each, so that every exchange can be assigned the correct share of all the interviews. Following that, the computer will take over by doing something very much like tossing a lot of numbers up in the air and letting them fall at random in groups of four. The muddle ends up with a list of phone numbers—the assigned three-digit exchanges plus the randomly selected four-digit numbers. Then, while the interviewers sit back and file their nails or fantasize about the day when they can get better jobs, the computer does the dialing. We were organized more or less like that to cover the whole state of New Hampshire from our Manchester headquarters.

It's even better than going through a phone book, because this way we could get the unlisted as well as the listed phones, what with the computer grabbing numbers from the sky. If you yourself have an unlisted phone and you should one day get a call asking you what brand of cat food your pet is least likely to turn her whiskers up at, don't bother to ask how the survey people got your number; the gods of statistical chance snitched on you; there's no hiding place down here no more.

And that's not all. After the phone is answered, the screen in front of the interviewer, a screen much like your TV set, flashes instructions as to whom the interviewer should try to speak to—ma, pa, auntie, or whomever.

That doesn't end it, either. Next, the computer controls what the interviewer will ask. Suppose the question flashed on the screen is, "Are you married, single, widowed, or divorced?" and you, a comely eighteen-year-old coed, admit to the single state. The interviewer taps out an S on the keyboard. This signals the computer automatically to skip the next question, which is, "How many children under thirteen do you have?" (You tramp.) Real live interviewers sometimes forget to skip, in the heat of the battle, and indignant maidens of high birth have been known to fly into a tizzy, sensing insult, and to terminate the interview abruptly by slamming down the receiver.

As the interviewers tap out the answers onto their keyboards, the machinery gobbles them up and blends them all together. Once that is accomplished—and it takes no time at all—if you want to know how your candidate, or any other candidate, is doing with people who have kids under thirteen, a couple of properly tickled buttons will get the results spewed forth by a high-speed printer for your consideration.

There's no way to make the interviewing process more foolproof, short of giving lie detector tests to survey respondents if you're in any way suspicious of their answers.

I briefed the kids on the questionnaire, which was a general attempt to parallel the national studies on issues like taxation, deficits, and relations with Russia, plus some local topics for the Northeast like acid rain and the drain of industry to nonunionized areas of the country. And of course I put in that personal integrity item that poked its head up in Iowa.

The dialing setup was such that if there was no answer after five rings the computer would cluck irritably and slip that number to the bottom of the pile, to be tried again at a different time of day; people with different jobs or different life-styles keep different hours, but they must still be interviewed. The interview clocked out at ten minutes, but what with time lost on dialing, no answers, and respondent refusals to talk to us, plus some leeway for the interviewers to come up for air, I was counting on four completed interviews per hour per interviewer. Not much in itself, but when two days' results were combined, you began to get something usable. I was thinking about using the moving average principle, that is, adding together day one and day two results, then dropping day one and combining day two and day three, and so on until the end of time or the end of the campaign (and if you've lived through many campaigns there may not appear to be much difference between the two). Questions would be deleted or added according to the needs of the moment, though I intended to ask about the personal integrity issue until everybody was satisfied that the results were no longer flashing warning signals—if that day ever arrived.

The solitary desk along the fourth wall of our interviewing room had a telephone monitor on it so that we could tune in on the interviewers at random to check out how they were doing.

After the briefing session, I dismissed the gang until five. Delaney then suggested that I drop over to campaign headquarters with him to check in with the candidate. Bill and Betty were to be there too, as well as McGrath's family, daughter Eileen and son George.

"George just blew in. To help Daddy, for God's sake!" Delaney said. "You haven't met him yet, have you." He wasn't asking a question, but uttering a cry of despair.

"No. What's he like?"

"Like nothing else around, thank God. He doesn't think he's the candidate's son, oh, no, not that one. You know how a small kid can be when he's pissed off at his folks? Figures he's really the king's son, stolen from the cradle by gypsies and dumped on some peasant's doorstep?"

"Story of my life, Al."

"Yeah. Well, this kid has never stopped believing it, even at age twenty-two or thereabouts. Daddy's got clout, and the young prince is out to cash in on it. Doesn't work, says he wants to find himself, if you can swallow that line. Throws his weight around, trouble with women, drinking, what all.

"Eileen gets worse press because she sounds off a lot. Riles people up, but I'll take ten of her to one of her baby brother. Listen," he said, hotting up to the topic, "that royal prince ever tried knocking on the door at Buckingham Palace the queen'd take one look and tell him 'Fuck orf, sonny.'" He shook his head.

"Oh. You mean you don't like him."

"Hell, doesn't matter. So long as he doesn't screw things up for Johnny, which may be asking too much. Let's leave it that he's a pasty-faced punk who's so used up he looks fifty, and then let's forget him. Okay?"

"If it's okay with you."

"It's okay with me." We started walking faster, the New Hampshire air frosting in front of our mouths and probably hanging from our eyelashes. My feet were cold, though Jane had packed me woolen socks and I had brought along the heavy hiking shoes. Cold was the beginning, middle, and end of all reality. I stomped my prints into the fresh snow; there was, I realized sadly, always fresh snow to stomp prints onto, except where there was slippery ice to crash bottoms onto.

Half a block of silence and Delaney was revved up again. "But that Eileen's a doll. She's going to be a help, no matter how much the yahoos yap about her. Tough and honest as they come; that's why so many people can't stand her, I guess."

Campaign headquarters had enough ringing phones and shouting volunteers to drown out a Wagnerian soprano, had there been room for one in the room, which there wasn't. There was an overabundance of battered desks and chairs, boxes of buttons and pamphlets, posters on the grimy buff walls, and too many people, maybe fifteen, in a space for ten, charging around sufficiently to take up room for thirty.

"Hey, boy," McGrath greeted me, "you set to go? We need all the help we can get. Somebody's flooding the state with these damned handbills. Take a look." He shook a paper at me so agitatedly that I didn't get a look. "And oh, yeah, meet the family. Eileen, you know. This is George, my son. George, meet Ev Franklin, our pollster."

Half a second later than Emily Post would have liked it, George tore his eyes away from the hindquarters of a young lady bending over a carton on the floor. "Pleased to meetcha," he said, without emphasizing his pleasure to the point of extending a hand. Delaney was at least partially right; the boy was unhealthily puffy, with skin the texture of an abandoned lemon meringue pie. His face held the expression of a kid who got new underwear for his birthday instead of the electric train he had hinted for. And tiny, reddened eyes were reminiscent of the light on an electric appliance petulantly signaling the ON position.

Deliberately, I put out my own hand. He took it after another unnecessary fraction of a second. My mistake: I had the uneasy feeling I was shaking a flannel pancake, with syrup.

"Me too," I lied.

"All right," the candidate said, "let's get to it. There's no time for diddling around. I shouldn't even be here. The other boys will be making hay in Iowa while I'm diddling around with this trash in New Hampshire. Listen to this!"

He held the handbill up again with one hand and slapped it with the other. He peered testily through the bottom of his bifocals, a man resenting the inconvenience of middle-aged eyesight. "'How can a man who can't manage one American family manage a hundred million families?' And, 'Can this man serve as an example to your children? Is he fit to lead the greatest nation on God's good earth?'"

He snorted. "You wanna guess at the answers? And not a single outright lie in any of it. Look! They say a woman took a shot at me, that spaced-out freak in Iowa. They say she yelled that I knocked her up, promised to marry her. True, that's what she said. So what do I do, spread it around some more by denying it?

"Here's a different one." He picked up a second sheet. They're going after the kids and their mother. The whole family. Nobody says I drove Paula to drink, oh no! They just ask who's responsible. They ask if I deserted her. What do I do, say, sure, she's on the sauce, but don't look at me? And George's two arrests for drunken driving, one time breaking some goddamned kid's leg."

He whipped his glasses off and shook them at us, like a medicine man exorcising an evil spirit. "How the hell do they get all this stuff? It's like they had a graduate student doing library research on me full time, for God's sake! And—"

"Come on, Dad," George protested, more concerned about himself. "That kid ran out in the street between two parked cars, right smack—"

"Shut up," the candidate snapped. "That's not all about you, son. You shot your mouth off to some reporter how you'd never take a regular job until you found yourself, didn't you? Found yourself, for God's sake!"

"Wait a minute, that guy tricked me, and all I was trying to say to him was—"

"All you were trying to say was that you're an idiot," Eileen broke in, her fists clenched and her frame rigid with fury. "Believe me, George, if you ever find yourself, you know what? You won't like it, that's what!"

"Oh, you're terribly funny," her brother shot back. "And how about you, angel, what's to like about you, dropping your drawers in half the bedrooms in Orange County."

Eileen's right fist snapped up as if on a spring and

headed toward her brother's face. McGrath slapped it down. "Cut that out," he ordered. "We've got trouble enough." He sagged. "The devil with it, all of it. What's it matter, anyway? The hell with it." He balled up one of papers in front of him and shot it at the wastebasket, missing.

"I'll tell you what it matters," Delaney replied. "It matters that you can't let this get to you, Johnny. You've got to get something underway, and right now." He pointed a cigar at me and the others, as if we were jointly responsible for whatever Johnny, his wife, and his kids had or hadn't done; now it was up to us to make amends.

"Look, Johnny," Betty suggested, "we'll get character statements, endorsements from ministers, priests, rabbis—the whole schmear."

"Fine," Johnny said, not looking as if he really thought so. "That's why I'm here. I've already got meetings set up with political clubs in Manchester, and if you can work in some religious groups, and get me into Concord and Nashua and Portsmouth—oh, hell, I don't know how I'm supposed to cover it all. Look at this garbage! And I ought to get up to the northern part of the state somehow. Al, maybe you can work out something." He shook his head. He sounded weary. "How'm I going to get it done? How the bloody hell am I going to get it done?"

"You get it done, and we'll get you coverage," Betty assured him.

"We'll work in some ads, too," Bill said. "You a member of the American Legion? Pictures with one of those hats go great."

"And I'll be tracking it in the polls to see how we make out," I put in.

"Okay," the candidate agreed dubiously. "I'll have to count on you all. And remember I've got to get back to Iowa as soon as possible. And I wonder what else they're up to, whoever they are, besides this pack of lies. How do they do it? How do they dig it all up?" If candidates for high office were allowed to cry, Johnny McGrath might have squeezed out a few tears. Instead, he glared at his watch and said, "I've got to get out of here." He kissed his daughter lightly, nodded to the rest of us, and strode out the door.

"Take care, Dad," Eileen called after him.

A brief silence was broken by George, who asked, "Say, about this tomato who took a shot at Dad in Des Moines, you maybe got a file I could look at?" He gave a rueful grin of admiration. "Who'd have thought it of the old man?" About the only normal thing George shared with every other kid in the world was the firm conviction that his parents had long since forgotten whatever inadequate and joyless knowledge they had ever had of the sexual act.

Delaney looked at him in disgust. "What I like most about you, George, and believe me, it's a difficult choice, is your sense of the priorities." He shoved a thumb toward a file cabinet. "Look in there. Under Fuck," he advised. "You don't find it there, try Iowa. We got work to do."

The boy found what he was after and sat down, his back to the room. He bent over a file folder.

Delaney turned to Betty, Bill, and me. "Okay," he said, "you get the idea. We take the high road and ignore the specifics of this crap about Johnny and the family. We come down heavy on him as an earnest, dedicated, moral, family man—that American Legion gambit's a good one—and we let that do the trick. We hope. At the same time we don't lose sight of the big picture. We know the national issues, and the local boys know the local ones. Ev keeps track of how we're doing, and if any new trash floats to the surface, maybe he can spot it for us."

"I'll do what I can," I said, using words of modesty that would have gotten me canned on Madison Avenue.

"The candidates will be all over the landscape here in a week and a half, two weeks, and we've got to have

Johnny's local program blocked out by then. Right now, I want to get together with Betty and Bill and the local club to see how—"

"Keerist!" came a shout from across the room. Young George stood up and slammed shut the folder of clippings he was wading through. He turned his gummy face toward us without speaking and then spun about and strode out of the room, his dewlaps shaking with each step he took. "Holy shit!" he said as he passed through the door.

"What's the matter with Junior?" Betty asked.

"Who knows," Delaney said. "Probably late for his penicillin shot. Eileen, I wish we could have kept your brother out of this."

"I know. I do, too," Eileen said. "He wants to help but he's not going to. Dad keeps hoping, so that's it."

"Okay, let's skip it and go to work," Delaney said.

I started to head back to the motel so I could think about the next wave of interviewing. As I went through the door I heard poor Bill ask, "Did you mean that about the kid's penicillin shot? About his being late, I mean."

Poor Bill.

❑

NINE

❑

I hadn't planned on extra surveys, at least not this early in the game, but with so much riding on the personal integrity angle, I decided to go into high gear. High gear costs money. The budget was tight, what with Finch, Rowan, & Hyde in this partly on spec in the hope of getting the big account four years from now. I figured I'd better check in with the throne of St. Edward up there on the top floor on Madison Avenue.

"Well," Jorgensen conceded ungraciously, "if you think so. But don't spend a mint. We haven't landed the big one yet, you know. Go ahead then, if you must." Pharoah letting me know that even if there wasn't any money in the till for straw he still expected tomorrow's bricks delivered on schedule. Of course, he wasn't really all that naive. He knew his staff had to order the steak dinners when they were on the road, and order them in the best place in town, because biting down on the tuna surprise in unknown beaneries in strange cities is all too likely to lead to further surprises at three in the morning. And a boy and his dog, even a boy and his portable cassette player, are more separable than an ad man and his martini.

Put simply, in advertising, no matter what the job, there is no way money can be saved. Period. In fact, trying to save it usually costs. I can't speak for other businesses, but on Madison Avenue there are three ways to handle injunctions from on high to cut down on expenses. First, you can ignore them and spend more. This works beautifully, but, sad to relate, only for artists, writers, and TV commercial producers, the glitz and glamour of their overspending establishing them among the ultissima of free creative geniuses. Sometimes they even get raises that way.

There are only two courses for drones like me. The first is to farm the work out to another organization. This is complicated. Everyone normally charges his work time against the accounts he's on, and submits a time sheet periodically. His hourly wage is multiplied by three by the accounting office to cover salary, overhead, the costs of vacation and sick leave time, bonuses, health insurance, rent and equipment, taxes, miscellaneous, and finally, profit. The agency hasn't spent all this in out-of-pocket funds, but that's the world of accountancy; spend a buck's worth of time on a job and it ends up three bucks on the books.

Therefore, if you want to keep expenses down, you contract the work out. Let someone else do the typing, Xeroxing, interviewing, and processing of the data. They'll charge a normal profit, but they won't multiply by three. You end up spending more real money, but it comes out that you've saved a bundle, at least on the books.

That path wasn't open to me either, not here, anyway. I already had the donated services of a computer company and an interviewing staff. Everything that could be farmed out was already farmed out.

I took the third way, as Big Ed damn well knew I'd have to: I stuck it to other accounts. Does the dog food budget have a cushion? Sock it to 'em. Is the cake mix client loaded? Let 'em eat McGrath. Simple. That's why the rule in advertising is that anybody who brings a job in under budget is a fool: There *must* be something you can use it for rather than let the client get away with all that nice, warm cash. When I spoke to Jane that night I asked her to look the books over and find me a couple of fat pigeons for roasting. I also told Betty and Bill about the problem so they could pull their strings for fudging the charges. I don't know who their marks were, because it's not manners to ask.

The three of us worked around the clock, as did Delaney and his people. It paid off. The candidate spliced some suggested references to the Almighty and to his special love for his children into his speeches in the East and then back in Iowa, and our team plastered these golden words the admittedly modest length and breadth of New Hampshire. Betty Gold and Al Delaney must have found every man of the cloth willing to go for a little publicity. If there had been any Shinto priests in New Hampshire at least one of them—saffron robes gorgeous on color television—would have been saying something sweet about Johnny McGrath.

At first the upward ticks in the negative impression of the candidate's personal integrity continued, reaching 14 percent. Then it began to trend down, and in the course of the next week if found its way back to eight percent negative. Still too high, but a lot better. And from the reactions to the questions on Johnny's positions on foreign policy, social programs, budget deficits, and the rest of it, it looked like the man was not only saying the right things, but that he was saying them in a way people could understand.

They were starting to understand what he stood for, and they were liking it.

Johnny was still behind Havemeyer, which was where he wanted to be anyway, but he began to pull ahead of Bobby Leich. Duckworth slipped to fourth, and the others weren't even in the race. Even Ed Jorgensen should have been willing to admit that we were doing a hell of a job, though he never would. I intended, nevertheless, to raise the point in a modest manner when it was time to hit him up for a raise.

Naturally, it didn't last.

The candidates pulled into Manchester just past the middle of February. It was snowing. They arrived on different days, and at different times of the day, but whenever they got there it was snowing. It was a winter when anybody in love with beautiful white New England churches and white New England homes would have been well advised to admire them on calendar pictures. To view them in the flesh was to view them through eyes that stung and teared or through eyeglasses opaque with frost. It was a winter to keep a handkerchief permanently at the ready, together with a legion of back-up tissues jammed into every pocket. It was a winter that expressed its disdain for primary campaigns and for the people who perform in them, from the lowliest spear carriers to the leading tenors. It was a winter that hated everybody over twelve.

The camp followers and the nuts swarmed in from Iowa like a locust plague. Some of them looked as if they couldn't have afforded the plane fare, and from some samples of their fanaticism I wouldn't have been surprised to learn that they had walked. And the voice of the cuckoos was heard throughout the land—from the right, left, and center.

The madness spread like fungus in a basement apartment in Savannah. At one extreme, I saw a sign advocating the death penalty for abortionists (because they killed people, no doubt), and at the other end of the spectrum I had a handbill thrust into my unwilling hands calling for reverse discrimination in the armed forces until women equaled 50 percent of the nation's combat troops. Sitting with Bill, Betty, and Al in our favorite greasy spoon, I commented too audibly that the delegate from the National Organization for Women seated in the next booth looked like "a hit man for the feminists to me."

Before a split second had ticked its way into eternity, the lady was standing over me. "Did I hear you right, Mac, what you said?"

"Uh, what?"

"That hit man bit. I heard, all right, didn't I?"

"Well, I, uh."

She jabbed a finger into my chest. "Not hit man, buddy. Hit person. And don't you forget it." Bursting into a cackle of satisfaction at having put me down, she thumped happily back to her own booth. She caught me looking at her. "And don't you forget it," she repeated.

Don't get the idea I'm trying to badmouth the feminists. Everybody was crazy. Among the conservatives, some equally special specimens were in high gear. There were the ladies over sixty in the right to life movement, the ones with plenty of time to trail after politicians and plump for causes since their own families were raised and out of the house. These blue-haired crusaders strode manfully through the local streets, braving the cold, with signs denouncing the feminists, and acting as if everybody who wasn't a blue-haired lady with a sign was an advocate of free love and fly-front trousers for women. They bore great plops of lavender body powder visible on their mottled chests like medals that proclaimed, along with the stale scent, that no matter how clean you considered yourself, and no matter when you had last scrubbed yourself down in the shower, they had personally bathed even more recently than you. They kept making me feel guilty. Even in the shower. Every time.

That's what Manchester was like that winter.

But those were just the innocent diversions. More serious business was afoot as well. The attacks on Johnny started up again with even greater ferocity and variety than the earlier efforts. A whispering campaign was in progress, and I was picking it up in my interviews. We called back some of the respondents who found Johnny lacking in that magic personal integrity, and talked to them without benefit of computer. I made some of the calls myself, asking, "What did you have in mind when you said you were uncertain about John McGrath's personal integrity?"

I'd get answers like, "Oh, I don't know, maybe not much, I guess, only it's like my husband heard at the plant about there was this woman. . . ." "Well, my wife was gabbing with the other hens at the beauty parlor, and the hairdresser, she said she heard from a friend that . . ." "I just don't like what I hear, that's all." "We was shooting pool last week, and this guy we know, he said . . ."

And that marvelous catchall that has ruined more lives than the lack of a highly advertised mouthwash that kills bad breath germs on contact for lasting protection: "Personally, I don't know anything about it, but it seems to me where there's smoke there's fire."

Where there's smoke there's fire, and we had smoke aplenty, far beyond the handbills of a couple of weeks ago. There was even a bogus copy of the *Dartmouth Review* making the rounds all across the state. The *Review* is a conservative publication put out by Dartmouth College students in Hanover, New Hampshire, and it carries a lot of weight, not only because it's so cleverly right of center when right of center is in fashion, but also because none of the team that edits it ever took a course in Question Marks 101. They're as certain of every word they put to paper as a

1930s Communist, and the results are impressive; Father knows best, even if he is nineteen years old. "Put your own house in order first, Mayor McGrath," one fake editorial thundered. "If your finger is on the lady, how can we be sure it will be on the button if the day should arrive?" it queried in a rare resort to the interrogatory form. (That's how you could tell it was a fake.)

Johnny's bad boy rating zoomed to 15 percent.

"No," the candidate said at one staff meeting. "It's not Vern Duckworth. It could be some of the cranks behind him, but where the devil is their money coming from? This is a big operation."

"You know, Johnny, Duckworth either makes it in New Hampshire or he's through," Delaney said. "And it sounds a lot like his high moral baloney."

"Yeah," McGrath said grimly, "just like me. He either makes it here or he doesn't make it. I'll tell you why it isn't Ducky. He's a cynical old bastard, but he's even got himself fooled, in my opinion. He wouldn't think he had to resort to dirty tricks to get what he wants. He's parlayed religion into something as big as General Motors, and he's innocent enough to think he's the smartest kid on the block. He doesn't need dirty tricks, would be how I'd guess he's thinking, and he's been around long enough to know they could backfire."

"Yeah, if we're lucky," Al Delaney said, his face as solemn as I'd ever seen it, the round cheeks sagging into his wattles.

"I haven't understood half of what you're saying," I said.

Betty and Bill agreed: "Sounds like doubletalk to me." "Run through that again, huh?"

"I can't. It's my gut feeling, and that's the best I can do," McGrath said. "Look how Vern's been talking. Look at his speeches. Listen to the man. Nothing much about the issues, only about the purity of his views. He's shrewd enough to know he's ignorant. Oh, maybe he's shown a little knowledge—not too much—of domestic politics beyond simple questions of morality. But get to the international scene, he's totally lost, doesn't have an idea in hell what's going on, so he damns them all for being un-American. Vern probably thinks Tito was some kind of dog in the Wizard of Oz.

"That's the whole point I'm trying to make. He's not unintelligent, Lord, no, but he figures he's so damn smart he can skip the preliminaries and hasn't got any need to play dirty tricks on a dumdum like me." He sighed. "I guess I can't explain it. Let's leave it that Vernon Duckworth deep down believes he's smart enough to get away with being stupid."

"Well, you've lost me," Delaney admitted, "but let's move on. If not Duckworth, who? Leich? We were neck and neck with him until you pulled ahead last week."

"It's a possibility. We don't love each other much. But I doubt it. Too early in the campaign for him to feel desperate enough for that kind of crap."

"Then what do we do? How do we find out? Do we *want* to find out?"

Nobody stirred. Nobody except Bill Toscani, who looked around with creases in his handsome brow, almost certainly longing but not daring to ask What do we do about finding out about *What*?

TEN

Somebody had done three bags full of research on John McGrath, three garbage bags full. They had all the dirt, they knew the innuendos and the half-truths that would stick, and what may have been funny as all get-out to some warped character, they must have known that any attempt to deny it directly would only spread it further, the way rubbing at a grease spot on clothing drives it in deeper and wider. Daughter Eileen's stud farm was numbered and named, everything told except measurements; son George's careening in the fast lane was amply detailed; and if the brand of rotgut preferred by ex-wife Paula was left out, it was only because they were probably saving it for later issuance.

At one of the meetings of the candidates, Johnny addressed the problem squarely and requested that they all make sure their own troops weren't the responsible agents. They sympathized and deplored mightily, and may even have been sincere, but it was clear that they regarded Johnny's troubles as one of the risks of the game. "Fortunes of war, son," Havemeyer observed contentedly, "fortunes of war. We all go through it."

That wise old pro Al Delaney knew before the candidate himself did that there wouldn't be any help forthcoming from these boys. He assembled the Finch, Rowan, & Hyde team. "Look," he told us, "the only thing to do is dig up the dirt ourselves before somebody else does it for us. We've got to know the worst that can happen so we don't get caught by surprise."

"How's that going to help?" Betty asked. "If McGrath has dipped into the wrong pair of bloomers, what's the difference if we know about it before somebody else broadcasts the details?"

"I don't know," Delaney admitted. "But you remember some years ago some guy wanted to be vice-president, and it came out he had had a round of sessions with a psychoanalyst? So what? I mean, analysis is pretty ordinary these days. No big deal. It's so far in it's out. But his own team didn't know about it, so when the opposition found out they made it sound like this nice, handsome, clean-cut boy from the Middle West, he had done something dirty, sex fantasies about his momma, maybe. It ruined his chances. They never could get things in one piece again. Maybe if his bunch had known beforehand? Maybe they could have been ready?" He shrugged his shoulders. "I dunno, but maybe. See what I mean?

"Okay," he went on, "so I'll take Johnny on myself. You characters get hold of the two kids and pump them for everything they know or think they know that could make their old man smell funny. Hit them one at a time because if you get those two together all you'll get is a fight." He looked at his watch. "It's three now, just about time for

George to be starting his precocktail hour cocktail hour. Why don't you see if you can spot him in the bar? Then maybe after that you can get Eileen out to some quiet place for dinner and see what she can give you. Okay?"

We agreed to meet later, or the next morning if the dirty stories went on too long. I went to the bar to look for George while Betty hunted up Eileen to line her up for dinner. I think Bill went to his room to play with his building blocks or to take a nap for quiet hour or something.

George was in the bar, as Delaney had predicted. He was in a booth with two men twice his age. One of the men had a nose that looked to be broken and listing to port, at least one cauliflower ear, and a cigar growing out of his mouth. Definitely not Ivy League. The other was a less impressive version of the same, with pale, watery eyes, the kind that befit a heavy drinker, and a toothpick growing out of his mouth. Unless it was a battering ram. They were in more serious conversation than I had previously imagined young George capable of. I stepped over. "I'm sorry to interrupt, gentlemen," I said, "but I have to speak to George here on a serious matter. It's about the campaign, George, and I need your help. Your father needs it, I mean."

The boy looked doubtfully at one of his companions, the toothpick, who in turn looked at the other one, the cigar. Cigar frowned, digested my request, then gave a what-da-hell gesture of indifference. "Sure thing," he said. "See you later, kid." He raised an arm to flag the waitress. "Bring my father here the check," he told her, and turning to George, he added, "Your treat, hey, kid?"

The waitress took a twenty from George. When she brought the change, cigar picked it up, peeled off two bucks for a tip, and pocketed the rest. "Thanks a lot, kid," he said to George. Both men laughed, and when they did I knew that I had seen them before. They were the two who had found it so kicky that day in Des Moines when a gun had been fired at John McGrath. Some lucky people can find a bright side to anything, I suppose. I tentatively put them down as part of somebody else's campaign, though what they would be doing with George I couldn't figure. Or maybe they were campaign followers, buddying up to anybody in the center of the action. Or maybe not. There was something wrong here, I was sure, but what it was I wasn't sure. I hate to sound snobbish, but those two didn't look the type to be interested in politics for its own sake; permanently embedded cigars and toothpicks never did seem to me to indicate a concern with unemployment rates, foreign debt, or third world suffering.

Once outside, I said to George, "I want to talk to you about your father's campaign. Let's get in my car and go somewhere away from the crowds." He agreed. I navigated into the countryside where the roads were sufficiently empty for me to relax and turn my attention to talking with George. "Who were those two guys, George?"

"Just two fellows I met," he said. "We got to talking, like. You know?"

"Seemed to me that guy was making pretty free with your twenty back there. I mean for just a couple of guys you got to talking with, like."

"We had a bet, that's all. He won. Look, Ev, I've got this date tonight. What do you want to talk to me about?"

It was reasonably clear what George *didn't* want to talk about. I dropped it. "About this smear campaign against your father. I want to lay a couple of questions on you. See what you can tell me."

"What would I know about that? You think I've got something to do with it, don't you?" His voice rose to a whine, and though I had never heard it before, I knew that it was a characteristic whine—high, thin, and unpleasant, a voice that goes with a runny nose. "My own father, for God's sake! Cut it out, that's all. Anything goes wrong it gets pinned on good old George." He swiveled toward me. "Eileen put you up to this, didn't she? That bitch."

"Shut up, kid," I said wearily. "Just for half a second, shut up and listen."

"Yeah," he replied. "'Shut up, George. Listen, George. It's all your fault, George.' I'm tired of that shit! Anything goes wrong, it's George's fault!" He got even shriller. I took my eyes off the road and looked at his screwed up features. That pudgy face was a wax model of a pudding, boneless and beginning to melt under the assault of some inner heat. "You're all gonna cut it out, you hear me?" he bellowed, and then turned toward me, one fist raised over his head like a high school girl about to throw a ball.

He slammed it down hard on my shoulder, and my hands twisted in reaction. We skidded. The tires protested in a squeal not unlike George's. I pulled over to the side of the road, shaking with shock, and stopped.

I couldn't have spoken over a whisper if I had wanted to, and I didn't want to. "You do anything like that again," I said through my teeth, "and I will beat the living hell out of you. I will dropkick your fat ass all the way to Kansas City without you bouncing once short of Bucyrus, Ohio. You understand me?"

We stared at each other. He looked frightened. I was frightened too, a middle-aged sack of martinis facing a boy half his age, even if the kid was as flaccid as a ball of dough. I contrived to look mean, though, and apparently I did it successfully, most likely a result of my many years of psychological warfare on Madison Avenue. A rancid tear gathered in the corner of George's eye and coursed round the curves of his puffy cheeks. "I'm sorry," he mumbled.

"Okay, now let's forget it and start all over. What I want to know has nothing to do with you," I said, though his outburst made me wonder if maybe it did indeed have something to do with him. I explained what the problem was, in more or less the same way Al Delaney had put it.

"And let me have it all, George, even the things you're not sure of. The works, everything they can throw at your father. We'll worry about what's true and what isn't some other time."

George wasn't stupid. He only looked, behaved, and talked stupid. He got the point. "Sure," he said, "but you know that after my folks broke up I lived with my grandma, Dad's mother. I didn't see too much of him except when he'd come over to St. Jo and visit."

"All right, but you've seen enough of what's been going on. The handbills, the rumors. You've got to know something about it."

"Not much. Honest. Except they got one thing dead wrong. A flat out lie. Dad had nothing to do with my mother starting to drink. I mean, even if anybody thought he treated her bad or gave her a lousy deal or something. Because she didn't start drinking until afterward, after they broke up and she went back to live with her father. As soon as I was old enough to understand, my grandmother told me. There was this other guy she got engaged to down there after the divorce—"

"Down where?"

"Down near Excelsior Springs. That's out of Kansas City. On her dad's farm. I think the fellow had some kind of agri business, a farm supply store, something like that. Anyway, they got engaged and then this bastard chickened out, and there was Momma with her bare face hanging out and all the locals getting lots of yaks out of it. It must have been pretty damn tough, and that's when she started to hit the bottle." He looked as if he was going to cry again. "Listen," he protested, "you live in some little dump like that and some guy does that to you and everybody inside of hooting distance knows and they've got nothing better to do than shoot their mouths off, and—"

"George, George, relax. Nobody's saying anything about your mother, or even about your father, for that matter. I'm just trying to understand what's been going on, that's all. Now what you've said could be important; we've caught a great big lie. I don't know what use we can make of it, not yet, but it's all grist for the mill if we keep on trying. Somehow we're going to bust up all these lies about your father, if we just keep working at it. You see? Now that's a great start. Let's see what else you maybe know."

"I don't know anything, not really. I mean, there I was living with Grandma most of the time, except when I'd go to visit Momma or Dad in the summer, when school was out. Once at Dad's place, there was this lady there, I guess his girlfriend, but I don't know a damn thing about it." His voice trailed off.

"Any of the kids around your father's place ever say anything to you about that?"

"Nothing. Not really. About my ma, though, one kid one time said something about how she had a gin bottle in her pocketbook. I asked my grandmother what that meant, and that's when she told me about this bastard who broke off with her." For a moment the boy looked defiant, but then his face sagged into its more natural state of dejection. "I guess I'm not much help. Ask Eileen. I think she'll be able to help more. She lived with Dad back then because she was in school when the folks broke up, and when Momma left town, they didn't want to drag Eileen out or something like that."

I tried more questions, but nothing sparked a response. What George knew, the little he knew, I had. After his outburst, my feeling was that the flood waters had swept the poisons away and that he was telling me everything as well as he could. He just didn't know very much about either of his parents. I took him back to the motel. I think he felt he had failed some kind of test, but there was nothing I could do about that. Even if I had wanted to, I mean. I had trouble enough with my own insanity without taking on this kid's as well.

On to Eileen. I found a message at the motel to call Betty. I did that and she told me we had a date to meet Eileen at seven for dinner. That gave me a couple of hours, so I went back to my room via the ice machine and scraped up a cardboard bucket of cubes. Once in the room I erased the memory of my outing with George by climbing into the tub with the ice, a glass, and a bottle of scotch on the bathroom floor beside me. Scotch is how I know I'm on the road: Martinis call for too much equipment; scotch requires only a bottle, a glass, and a bathtub for resting the weary mind and muscles. I took a sip, snuggled down in the warm water, shut my eyes, and pretended there were apple trees growing down the middle of Madison Avenue.

ELEVEN

Eileen McGrath was a tougher customer than her baby brother, so Betty and I decided to play it cool by making the occasion a semisocial one rather than a third degree. We piled into the car as two couples out for the evening—Bill and Betty, Eileen and me—and headed for a quiet restaurant in Concord that someone had recommended. At least it would be away from the political crowds at the better places in Manchester, and maybe it would relax us all.

Once at the table, Betty primed herself with a couple of drinks and put it to the girl: "We don't *want* to know, dear; we've *got* to know, if we're going to be able to help your father. We can't afford to sit around and wait, and then find out about the skeletons in John McGrath's closet from some slander sheet. We need the dirt in advance, all of it, and you're the only one who can let us have it. All of it," she repeated, "and don't hold back. Right down to the last back alley affair—if there was one, I mean."

At first, as we had feared, the firmer Betty's monologue got, the firmer got Eileen McGrath's uncooperative chin. A quarter of an hour of getting nowhere and Betty belted back the dregs of her drink and signaled the waiter for a third. "There goes the last of my waistline. Again," she said grimly. "To hell with it. Well, how about it, kid? We can't crap around forever. Are you going to help your old man or are you going to sit around and watch him get creamed? Personally I don't give a goddamn anymore, so just tell me what it's gonna be."

The chin jutted forward and then settled back, like a retractable cannon. The lips parted, but nothing came out. At last, the girl said wearily, "Okay, okay. I get the picture. Let me think a minute. It all stinks and I need to get my head straight before I start. I don't much like talking about it, either, I can tell you that, so we do it my way or we don't do it, understand?" It struck me that somewhere in the middle of the flaming unconventionality that was Eileen McGrath's trademark, there was a right proper schoolmarm with her hair pulled back in a bun, stiff with disapproval of all us sinners. Tugged in two directions at once, no wonder the girl was so uptight.

She leaned back frowning, chewing on her lower lip. Her hand was wrapped around a scotch and soda as if she fully intended to squeeze the evil out of it—and as if she could undoubtedly succeed. "It's hard to know where to begin," she said hesitantly. "The worst anybody can get hold of is what he did to my mother. It's like a cheap novel. Two small town kids get married. He grows, she doesn't. He learns to eat raw oysters, she thinks they're only for shoving in the Thanksgiving turkey. Do you get what I'm saying? Finally he lets her have it: She's a drag on his career, and he wants out. She says no, he says yes, she starts drinking. He's no help."

She fiddled with a plastic swizzle stick until it snapped in two, and she looked at it disapprovingly, as if it were morally flawed. I remember wondering if she was looking at it as if it were her father's neck. "The truth is," she went on, "I don't think he tried very hard to pull things together again for the two of them. George was too young to get the picture, but I was old enough to understand about the other women. Not woman, but women. The kids in school made sure I heard about it. And anybody who really wanted to dig up the dirt could find out about Mother being trussed up like a barnyard animal, screaming loud enough to raise the whole town, and carted off to some so-called hospital with bars on the windows. Dead drunk to the world half the time. Hell, they practically had bulletins posted in the local supermarkets. Everybody knew about it, or thought they did. Maybe the whole damn state knew, for all I know. A real life drama, much better than soap opera."

She looked up from her drink, the remains of the swizzle stick, and from her shredded napkin. She stared at Betty. "You know, he didn't visit her once after the first month or so. And he wouldn't let me see her, much less George. It was supposed to be too upsetting, but I think that meant upsetting for him, not for Mother or us kids. Anyway, maybe you'll have to get ready to see that coming up in your handbills—'Candidate drives wife to drink and tosses her in the funny farm.'

"Then there was the divorce. Naturally," the girl said bitterly, "he couldn't afford a wife who was a dead weight on his career. Oh no, little Paula Beeler from Excelsior Springs wasn't good enough anymore. Maybe somebody could say now that she couldn't afford a husband who was a drag on her whole life, but nobody thought of that then. Maybe somebody'll dig up that case of the galloping gonads, too, because there was plenty of action. They got him in trouble with the wife of one of the town councilmen, and the stupid cow bought herself a divorce. But Dad didn't marry her. By then he was getting old enough to develop a taste for chicken, like the one who drew a bead on him in Des Moines."

She stopped talking and looked down at the table again, turning the fork over as if the manufacturer's mark was the encoded answer to some basic mystery. "That's about the worst that could come up, after what he did to my mother, this dancing in and out of half the beds in town, beginning even before my mother's breakdown. Now you've got it all, and I hope it's what you want.

"I guess there are some other things," she went on, "but they're the usual for any politician. Accusations that contracts went to his buddies, a school building that was so shoddy the plaster came down damn near as fast as they could patch it up. That sort of talk. I don't know what the truth is, but the stories are there for anybody who wants them. The local paper carried them, regular as Peanuts, until one of the big chains bought them out, and the new publisher, an old family friend, stopped it dead. But it's all in the files."

Sex being sexier than corruption, when it comes to scandal, I went back to what was more important. "What's with your mother now, Eileen?" I asked.

"You mean is she likely to do anything to embarrass him?" She cocked a cynical eye at me. "He needn't worry. She won't do anything or say anything. She plain isn't up to it. The only thing she wants is to be left alone. She functions these days by closing out the world, not by stirring up trouble. Sometimes I wish . . . I don't know what I wish."

We sat in gloomy silence for a moment, Eileen deep in her own thoughts and the rest of us wondering what those might be. Bill Toscani broke the spell. "I wonder," he mused thoughtfully. "I wonder whether the gigot d'agneau à la cuillère is made with fresh lamb or that frozen junk from New Zealand. I mean, lamb doesn't freeze at all well." (Always listen when an account man discusses food in a restaurant; he's used to ordering the best, and he *knows*.) I've never been able to figure out whether he said that deliberately to clear the air or merely out of his customary sweet simplicity, but whatever the motivation, it did the trick. The clouds lifted, the party brightened and sat straighter, and we ordered dinner. The gigot was delicious.

Eileen dredged up a couple of other items about various bodies and where they were laid to rest, but they mostly concerned her brother George, whose talents for getting into trouble were prodigious, more than I would ever have credited him with. It didn't depress the girl to talk about George, and I think she even enjoyed it, especially when the opportunity arose for her to utter such endearments as "drunken, irresponsible lardass." She was also evenhanded enough to throw in a few items on her own liberated existence, about which we already knew, but she was reasonably certain that there were no special stories that might inflame the retarded minds of readers of the *National Enquirer*. Not that her life-style couldn't provide the stuff of gossip and salacious speculation for those so inclined.

It occurred to me that her version of what happened between her father and her mother was at variance with her brother's, but we had put her through enough of a grilling for one day, so I let it lay. Besides, the way she told it, Johnny driving his wife to drink was more in accord with the accusations going around than was George's story of the drinking starting after the new boyfriend had done a cop-out on the lady.

We drove back to Manchester and left Eileen in the lobby. I invited Bill and Betty to my room to talk it over, but Bill wanted to call home and check on a kid who had been running a fever earlier in the day. Betty joined me. She was already afloat on the predinner alcohol she had employed to power her assault on Eileen, plus the wine with dinner. Nevertheless, always game for added experience, she asked for a drink. I poured us each a slug out of my ever faithful bottle, while Betty disappeared into the john.

Two minutes later she reentered the room. "God," she moaned, "but I hate bathroom mirrors. Especially the ones you're not used to. Ever notice? You think your own mirror at home tells all. Then you get to a different one, even in a dump like this, and it tells the rest of all. You can't win."

"So don't turn on the light. Wear a veil. I dunno."

"Funny. You know, Ev, I don't like that McGrath woman. There's something about her."

"Oh, come off it. She leveled with us tonight, and anybody could see it wasn't easy. I think it hurt her, if you want to know."

"Yeah? Well, I don't think it hurt her, if *you* want to know. You notice how she took out after both the boys, her father and her brother? You ask me, having you and me and Bill watch the hate bubbling out was what hurt, not bad-mouthing the others. You think maybe she's Miss Goody-Goddamn-Two-Shoes or something, sitting in a chintz rocking chair and knitting samplers? That's what you think, dummy?"

What I thought was that one very tipsy aging femme fatale was a shade jealous of another female still able to hit on all eight cylinders. What I said was, "First, sweetheart, you don't knit samplers; you cross-stitch them. Second, I haven't noticed you in a rocking chair with your tatting either, unless Al Delaney is some kind of handicraft, which I doubt."

"Screw you too."

"Come on, cool it, will you? You sure you're not just a little bit jealous? Hell, you've had your fun, and you're still doing okay. So relax, huh?"

She stared at me, open-mouthed. "You horse's ass! Is that what you think? You don't understand anything, my friend, so let me tell you a couple of things. In the first place, that chick's not a man-grabber; she's a man-hater. That means how she hates half the human race. She hates her father and she hates her brother, and if you ask me, the reason she doesn't marry the guys she's shacked up with has nothing to do with sexual equality. She just doesn't cotton to any formal recognition that some poor slob is a part of life she needs."

"I didn't ask you, Betty, and I'm not going to."

She ignored the interruption. "That's how I see it. And as for me, do you really, I mean, really, think I've spent most of my time skipping from one bed to the next? That what you think?"

I tried again. "Betty," I said, "cut it out. What I think is none of your damn business, and what you think the facts are is none of mine, and I'm not even a little interested in hearing about it. The only thing I'll tell you I think is that you shouldn't drink more than you can hold, not at your age. You should know better. Can we cool this now, huh? We've got work to do."

Like a tire with a slow leak, she deflated and sagged. "Oh, okay, that's the way you feel. But just let me tell you a couple of things. Then I'll shut up," she said quietly. "Gimme a drink." She flopped into the easy chair and wriggled into a comfortable position. "Jeez, I wish I had a belt I could loosen. Now, you shut up and listen."

As if I had been doing anything else. As if I had had a choice. "The hell I will. What do you think—"

"I said shut up. And listen. You get to me, Franklin, really get to me, you thinking I'm jealous of that young cooz, that I'm some kind of used-up bag who wishes she wasn't. Well, I'm not. Look: When I was maybe eighteen I was a chubby little beast, the way I'm getting to be now all over again, and somehow the word got around that old Betty Borgas—they called me Betty Bigass—would put out because that was the only way she could get a date. I don't know, but the number of times I was supposed to have lost what was laughingly known in those days as my innocence—well, it wasn't biologically possible." She cocked her head to the side quizzically. "Maybe if I'd had a wash and wear cherry. . . . The guys would tell each other they really made out like crazy because they were afraid they'd lose face in the locker room if they didn't talk that way. Even Limp Noodle Lieberman, the little son of a bitch who could've used a peanut shell for a jock. I found later he invented a whole piss pot full of lies about me, and—Oh, that's another story, I suppose." She burped.

I took advantage of the momentary cessation in the outflow. "Betty," I said sternly, "I don't care if you lost it on a subway turnstile. Don't tell me about it. You're drunk. You'll hate yourself in the morning if you go on like this."

"No I won't," she objected petulantly. "Anyway, here's the point. I got myself this reputation, and I sort of liked it. Sure, I screw around some, but not as much as anybody thinks, so I'm a sexpot with all the hard work left out. Without busting my balls, if I can use the expression."

"Here we go again," I complained to the ceiling. "No, dear, you can't. Not possibly. Anyway, I've got only two words for that heartbreaking story."

"Yeah?"

"Yeah. Al is one. Delaney is the other."

"So you've got a small point. Granted. I didn't say I was a nun, did I? I'm just not the hot-bloomers Betty I'm supposed to be. That's all." She seemed anxious to discuss it, probably forever.

"Doll," I begged, "please. What're you getting at? It's late."

"Okay, just gimme one more shot, and I'll tell you again, though I shouldn't have to, big boy like you." She poured a stiff slug of scotch for herself, dropped in a couple of cubes, and stirred it with a finger, which she licked off thoughtfully. After swishing a mouthful about the undoubtedly overheated interior of her face, she snuggled down into the chair again and said, "I'm only trying to get you to see the difference between me and the McGrath. I mean really appreciate the difference. We both got the reputation. Agreed. But how we got there is different as all hell. I like guys; she hates 'em. Remember that and don't mix us up again, or I'll, I'll, I don't know what, but I will."

"Okay, I believe you. Now go 'way."

"Right, right. I know when I'm not wanted. Just one more thing." She ignored my stage sigh. "I hope that the poor little girl you admire so much doesn't wear short shorts when she does all those swell California things like play tennis." She waited. "You not going to ask me why?"

"All right, Betty, why?"

"Because when she reaches for a high one, her balls, they could hang out the bottom." She gave a raucous laugh that sounded like a fender crumbling, lowered her chin to her chest and closed her eyes.

I walked over and lifted her head. I pulled one lid up and gazed into the dull opacity of a marzipan eyeball. I let it snap back and made my way to the bed. After considering whether I'd guzzled enough to get sick, I rejected the idea. Then I looked back at the visiting corpse and figured to hell with it. I shucked my clothes, staggered into my pajamas, and was sacked out in thirteen seconds.

TWELVE

It got worse. It fed on itself. It was as if someone had taken a lump of New Hampshire snow the size of a Ping-Pong ball and started it rolling down from the top of Mount Washington, and it grew as it rolled and rolled as it grew until the whole state was knocked flat by it. We may not have known what personal integrity meant, but whatever it was, the voters were becoming increasingly sure Johnny McGrath didn't have it.

"We're finished," the candidate said dully. "Leich came over yesterday and wished me luck, the bastard, and you know what that means." He snorted. "Then he's got the gall to sympathize with me about getting shot by that nut in Iowa, as if he's saying ain't it a shame, getting a hole in me, and for nothing. And that plummy platform voice of his!

'Does it still hurt, Johnny? Does it hurt much?' I think he's after my vote, so help me!"

"What'd you tell him?" Delaney asked.

"What could I tell him? I said it only hurt when he came around. I said it'd stop hurting after he dropped out of the race. He laughed. Not too much, though, the prick."

"Yeah," Delaney agreed. He turned to me. "Nobody has to plant stories anymore. They have a life of their own. Right now, if Johnny patted an orphan on the head he'd get himself arrested for molesting."

"We're in the hole," McGrath said. "Maybe we should pull it down over our heads. Eileen could get us a headstone."

"Uh," I said, "maybe this is a lousy idea, but—"

"I'm sure it is," Delaney interrupted, "but don't let that stop you. All our ideas are lousy. Let's have it."

"Right. The way I see it, if you fellows say we're finished, there's no point in any more of these piddling little surveys. Not if nobody's going to listen to what Johnny's saying anyway. So why don't we blow the whole bundle at once, go for broke with one big survey, and see what we can come up with. Find out what the voters really have on their minds, but in a big way. What's to lose? Maybe we'll find something out." It sounded weak, even to me.

"We know what they have on their minds," Delaney said. "Sex. Johnny's sex life. Like that."

"Sure," I replied, "and maybe that's going to beat him. But suppose he changes his style, suppose he forgets who's not going to like what he says and how he says it. If he comes down hard on the big issues, without waffling the way candidates figure they have to, suppose he figures screw whoever's put off by it—I mean, what's to lose?" I asked again.

"The election, since you ask," McGrath said dully. "That's what's to lose."

"So? You say it's lost anyway, no? But you fold now,

and that's not all you lose. You lose the next ten elections, including the one for school crossing guard back home. If anybody even lets you run. You're finished, or am I wrong? You're the experts, you two, so you tell me. Myself, I don't think you can afford to cave in, even if you know you're going to end up last. Not if you like an occasional meatball with your spaghetti, you can't. You haven't got a choice, that's all. Anyway," I added feebly, since I never know when to shut up, "that's the way it looks to me."

The candidate and his manager looked at each other. "It's true, John," Delaney said. I had never heard him call the man anything but Johnny before; that seemed important. "We pick up the pieces now, much as we can, or there won't be any left to pick up later. We go ahead like nothing is wrong, or you're through in politics. Don't get me wrong, maybe you're through anyway, no matter what you do, but if you don't do anything, you're washed up for sure."

"Save the pep talk, friend," McGrath replied. "I'm through, period. Maybe I better see about a Chrysler dealership back home."

"You do that," Delaney countered. "You do that and you'll be that guy nobody'll buy a used car from. Come on, man, snap out of it."

"Okay," McGrath said, with no enthusiasm, "to save my career as a used car salesman. I'll take the gloves off, beginning today. Do your surveys, if you want, Franklin, but don't ask me to go along if I don't like what they tell me. I'm sunk no matter what, so I'm playing this my way, strictly by ear."

"That's the way," Delaney said, clapping the candidate on the shoulder. "The big ones have always done it that way. Play the crowd like a piano, make 'em smile while they get their throats cut. Reagan, Kennedy, Roosevelt, they could feel the way to handle the voters." He winked at me, a signal that we'd face that problem when we got to it.

Here we go again, I thought. Just like advertising. The client lets me know that if I tell him what he doesn't want to hear, he'll decide I'm wrong, no matter what. I wondered again if it was time to move up to the apple orchard and start gumming away on the apples that were too good to let the buying public get hold of.

The Daitches assembled the interviewing staff in the meeting room. When I got there, the kids were joking and laughing, even more than usual. "What's so funny?" I asked.

"It's Barbara Jellthrop here," Josh explained. "Her family's up in North Conway, the other end of the state, and the computer pooped out their phone for a call tonight."

"And that's one interview I do myself," the young girl put in. "Give the folks a hard time. This'll knock them flat!"

"Sorry, but I've got to break in," I interrupted. "I haven't had a chance to tell Josh and Ginny yet, but we're not doing a survey tonight. Something's come up, and we'll be getting into a much bigger job, but I need a couple of days to work on the questions. So after this meeting I won't need anybody until four in the afternoon day after tomorrow. I'll explain it all then."

"Oh, good," the girl said, "I'll take off and go up home. I can tell the folks about it then."

"Sorry again, Barbara," I said, "but we'd have to scratch that interview if you do that. If the interviewer and the respondent knew each other we'd never be sure just how that would affect the answers. After all, who's about to tell the truth to his own daughter? You can see that."

"Yeah, I guess so."

"You can tell them about it later. Okay, sweetheart?"

A young fellow spoke up. "Could I ask you something, Ev?"

"Sure. Shoot."

"How come you people from New York always call everybody sweetheart?" There was a laugh.

"That's easy. So people will think we're from Hollywood." There was a bigger laugh. I'm not ashamed to admit it—I reach for laughs, and I'm especially grateful when I get them from the young, a species I'm not overly comfortable with.

I sent them all on their happy ways. The Daitches were grinning when we were alone. "What's up?" I asked. "I do something funny?"

"No, it's not you," Josh explained. "It's Barbara Jellthrop. Maybe you and she both think she's going to see her family in North Conway this weekend, but nobody else agrees."

"Then why say so?"

"Because this is New Hampshire, man," Ginny explained. "She's got herself a boyfriend in Manchester, and they'll probably go off somewhere. Nobody cares, not really, but this state's a little like one big small town. If she noised it around about her boyfriend, chances are some kind soul would be on the horn to her folks up north inside of ten minutes. They'll probably go off to Boston if he can get away from his job."

"Then why say anything at all? This story about going off to see her family. Why bother?"

"I told you. This is a small town, New Hampshire. You make the proper gestures and that's all you need, even if everybody knows it a lie. Besides, there are some cousins down here too."

"Oh," I said, "I see," not seeing at all. "That's too subtle for a simple city boy like me. I'll ask my wife about it when I go home next time. She's from a small town. Or will anybody believe me if I say I'm going home to see my wife and kid?"

"No."

"That's what I figured."

THIRTEEN

I headed for my room to work on the questionnaire, and fortified myself with several deliveries from room service. I eat too much at times like this, and I eat only the best. Maybe on some subconscious level I figure that steaks and crab meat and asparagus out of season and other such necessities will coax the creative juices to flow with greater abandon. Or, on the other, and more realistic hand, maybe I just like to eat for free on Big Ed Jorgensen. After all, experience has shown that I'm more likely to reach new frontiers in the waistline department than in the art of public opinion research.

Nevertheless, by midnight I knew I had a good thing going. In fact, I had too many good things going. There's a limit to how hard you can push people into answering a raft of questions about nuclear weapons, disarmament, farm subsidies, import restrictions, balanced budgets, aid to cities, tax reform, and everything else they ought to at least pretend to be interested in. Even if you get a professor of political science on the other end of the phone, you can't burn him out with endless probing. Somebody had to make decisions about what I could eliminate, and that somebody wasn't going to be me.

I broke a rule. I knocked on the candidate's door at one in the morning. He was generally up before six each morning, and never got back to his room before midnight. His routine was to ready himself for bed with no company except a couple of shots of bourbon, and then to crawl under the covers and turn his mind off as best he could. In silence. In solitude. If I had phoned he would have said it could wait for morning and what the hell did I mean by calling him at this hour, but by morning I knew I'd never be able to nail him to the floor long enough to get the decisions I needed. So I knocked.

As I did, I realized that the ordained silence and solitude were conspicuously absent. An angry Al Delaney opened up, snapping, "What the hell do you want?" even before he saw who was there. "Oh, it's you. Come on in. Join the fun. We're having a family crisis," he said bitterly.

Besides a pajama-clad Johnny McGrath vibrating midway between fury and despair, my eyes found a blazing Eileen, her fists clenched, the cords in her neck standing out, looking as if thunderbolts had just rocketed forth from her eyes. Then there was a highly fragmented George. More specifically, George's coat and shirt were in fragments, and that unlovely face appeared ready for the same condition if the lad were so foolish as to turn it into a strong wind. His lip was cut, his nose even redder and larger than nature had intended, and the blue-black of a telltale love tap had been hung beneath his right eye. Liberally dispensed daubs of mud enlivened the overall effect and completed the puffy facial decor for a gilding of the lily as horrible as it was redundant. A flap of skin was peeled back on his cheek to reveal the dull red flesh beneath, possibly to prove that George was truly human.

Three heads, if you count George's only once, swiveled in my direction and then turned back to their business, which was cat-fighting.

"You damn fool!" Eileen was barking. "How could you? You know what they're doing to Dad, and you still get sloppy drunk and tossed out of a bar. What's this, George, the fifth time this year or only the fourth?"

"With a full complement of reporters on hand," the candidate put in. "Or did you phone them after it happened?"

"Before it happened, maybe," Eileen offered. "He's stupid enough."

"For the last time, Dad," George whined, "I *told* you. I've been in this place maybe five, six times for a nightcap. They know me there, we get along fine, but out of nowhere these two guys jump me. Out of nowhere!" he repeated. "I swear to God." Protestations of innocence sat as convincingly on George McGrath as on a shoplifter who insists he has no idea how that second pair of pants worked its way onto his legs, over his duff, and managed to get itself zippered up.

"Sure, sure," Eileen agreed, "just a wee dram. Like out of a gallon jug, you mean. And the stink that comes out when you flap your lips is Lavoris, right? Oh, damn you, George!"

Sniveling having cut no ice, George swung into the attack. "You shut up," he suggested strongly. "You're a hell of a one telling anybody how to behave, the way you and your lover boys—"

"Listen, you little pig—" his sister began.

Someone pounded on the wall for quiet, but none of us even blinked. "Ah, do me a favor, will ya," George said, "and turn to shit!"

A stunned moment, and it was Eileen at bat again, her

voice now soft, though still harsh. "I guess I can't say that to you, can I? It'd be after the fact, wouldn't it? I mean, you've managed to do that already, haven't you," she went on, her voice commencing to rise again, "you stupid—"

"Stop it, both of you," the candidate said in a weary voice, his hands raised over his head. "There's nothing we can do tonight. Suppose you all get the hell out of here and we'll see about it in the morning. I need some sleep—if I can get any after this." He turned from his family to signal the end of the session and looked at me. "What is it now, Ev?" he asked wearily. "Can't it wait until morning?"

I hesitated. "If I can get hold of you, you and Al, for twenty minutes without interruption, yes. Otherwise, it's got to be tonight."

We arranged to breakfast in his room at seven. I went back to my own cell and called Jane. "This is a peachy time to call," she yawned, "or is it dawn in New Hampshire?"

"I'm sorry, love, but I'm setting up an all-out survey and before I talk about it to McGrath in the morning I really have to check with you. It's sort of the make or break point, and I need your help, okay?" I told her my problems and my ideas and she gave me a few more of the latter and dismissed a few of the former. Then I asked, "All in all, what do you think? Be honest."

"Franklin," she replied, "I'll be honest. I think two things. First, you're trying to get yourself fired, and second, you're absolutely right to talk the man into shooting the works. Of course, if it bombs, we could be upstate in a month walking barefoot through the apples."

"I hope we are," I said defensively. "Even if it is hard on the arches in March."

"I'm serious, sort of. If this goes well, you'll be brilliant. If it flops, well, at least maybe you'll be happy. Billy and I will get our new shoes every Christmas and we'll learn how to turn down thermostats to fifty at night. And if that doesn't kill us at least maybe it'll stun the cold germs. We'll all be the better for it."

"Yeah," I said without enthusiasm. "I guess I painted myself into a corner, huh?"

"I guess you did, but look, I don't seriously think anybody's going to sack you if it doesn't work out. From what you say, this boy's a certified loser no matter what, and besides, this is all apart from your main work at the agency. Even if it came to leaving this lousy job, which it won't, well, what the hell, kismet. We'll move upstate. I mean it. Honest. Billy would love it, you'd be happy, I'd bake pies out of the apples we couldn't sell until I could find something to do. I think I'm too old to be a hooker, but you never know. Stop quivering, Franklin. Like the kids used to say—*do it*!! Shut up and *do it*!!"

"I will. You're wonderful, you know?"

"I know. Now go to bed, sweetheart. It's late."

"Okay. Hey, don't hang up! One more thing."

"Oh, Ev, it's so late. What is it now?"

"Tell me something."

"Anything. Just let me get back to sleep."

"It's only that I was wondering why you people from New York always call everybody sweetheart."

There was a second's pause. The phone wires crackled expectantly. Then my rotten wife said, "Not everybody. Only special people. Like the guys whose names we can't remember." Then she hung up.

FOURTEEN

I tapped on the candidate's door early the next morning. Once again Delaney let me in, this time wordlessly. Eileen was there too, and she nodded mutely. McGrath ignored me completely.

The silence was catching, like being in church, and I spoke in sign language. I hefted two eyebrows, dangled one lip—the lower one—and turned my eyes from one to the next with, I suspect, the baffled appeal of a basset hound.

By way of answer, Delaney shoved the morning paper at me. George may have been physically absent from the room, but out of mind he was definitely not. There the lad was on page one, not as large as life, but at least as ugly. After the previous night's hassle the details were no surprise, but the picture of George on a sidewalk in front of a bar, sitting squat and dumpy in the posture that only drunks and infants can achieve when they try to hold themselves upright, was not without its novelty. There were trash cans beside him, and his battered face and torn clothing added an exquisite touch of authenticity to the scene. The bartender was quoted: George was drunk, annoying several of the ladies in the bar, and had to be, as the man put it in the words that are sacred ritual at moments like this, "forcibly ejected from the premises."

"It'll be on TV tonight," Delaney assured me, "for anybody who missed the original. The camera crews were there."

"How'd they do that, for God's sake? It couldn't have lasted sixty seconds, the whole thing. Less, even."

"Who the hell knows?" Delaney said.

"Who the hell cares?" the candidate said.

"Somebody probably called the media while George was warming up for the big event," Eileen suggested. "My brother is always good copy."

"And getting better with practice," Delaney added.

"Oh, let's not go over it again," McGrath said. "I'm sick of it. It's obvious. The whole thing was set up in advance. It doesn't matter, not any more. It's happened, so it's happened. If we can ride with it, fine, and if we can't, we can't. Finis. Okay?" He turned to me and spoke more briskly. "Ev, you wanted to see me. Let's get going. Breakfast is over there. Grab yourself something, sweet rolls and coffee. Juice." I nodded and went over to the table set up at the side of the room. "You've got your twenty minutes," he said to my back, "so let's hear it."

"All right, Johnny," I responded, my mouth full of doughnut. "I've got a whole raft of things I'd like to cover in the survey. They're all important, but if we kept everything in we'd have people on the phone for damn near an hour, assuming they wouldn't hang up, which they would."

"Right. You want me to cut things out, that it?"

"That's it. You go through this. Don't worry about how

I've worded the questions, unless there's something way out of line. The most important things you put three checks next to, the least important you can cross out. Anything you'd like us to go into if there's time, mark with two checks. Don't worry if there's not a mark next to everything. I'll know the blanks are one step up from the lowest priorities. Oh, yeah, if I've left anything major out, scribble a note about it. Want me to come back later?"

"No. Stick around. I'll get rid of this right now." He waved me over to Al and Eileen across the room, like he was shooing away a fly.

"What do you think you're going to get out of this survey deal?" Delaney asked. "A lot of hoo-ha. We already know what the problem is. People are beginning to think Johnny couldn't manage a pay toilet without stealing quarters to buy his kids cocaine. His personal life, that lousy kid, and yeah, you too, Eileen. That's the problem. Problems," he corrected. He looked morosely at the girl. "Not that I'm blaming you. Somebody's out to nail your father, and you're convenient. Not like your brother doing his damnedest to screw things up."

"You don't have to explain," Eileen said. "But Al's right, Ev. What can you expect from more surveys? Everybody's been surveyed to death already. I hate you getting Dad all keyed up when we know it's damn near hopeless. Let's face it." She poured herself a cup of coffee and stared at it as if she expected the brew to sprout tea leaves for reading by a neighborhood gypsy.

"Let me tell you," I said. "First, I'll be honest, for a wonder. I'm not sure I can accomplish anything. But there are a couple of long shots worth trying. I'll keep this simple: Just remember two words—undecided is one, and salience is the other. And remember two more words—New and Hampshire. Got it? Okay.

"Now. The idea is for Johnny to make it big in New Hampshire, and not worry about anyplace else for the time. That's what you've been saying, isn't it?" Delaney nodded. "Right. Well then, first, I want to find out in as detailed a way as we can afford to do it, what's on the local Yankee mind. If the locals think South Carolina should get one fat hydrogen bomb laid on them for every three textile mills that leave here for the South, we should know it so we can figure out how Johnny can use it, and to hell with the boys in the Sunbelt. If Johnny makes it here he can worry about them four years from now. You with me so far?"

"I guess," Delaney answered, his voice carrying the enthusiasm of a passenger on the *Titanic* agreeing to blow up his water wings. Eileen nodded dubiously too, still looking for the errant tea leaf in her coffee.

"I don't mean to overstimulate you kids," I commented, "but bear with me. Next, there's the anti-Johnny voters. Some people would never vote for John McGrath, no matter what he says. Suppose that every bishop in New Hampshire would still be against a man with that much scandal in the family even if he proposed hand laundering their canonicals for free the first Tuesday of every month. So we write off the bishop vote."

"Stop talking dirty," Delaney said with a wan smile. At least I was holding his interest.

"And at the other extreme, there's bound to be people who can't see their way to voting for anybody else but Johnny, no matter what. They may not even like him, but there's nobody they dislike less. They're stuck with our boy, and nothing he can say or do is going to lose their votes. We can forget about them too; they're in the bag.

"Now comes the important thing—the guy in the middle, the undecided voter, the one who can't make up his mind or who changes it every other day. We've got to make up his mind for him, nail him down in our camp. I'll make up an example, show you what I mean. There's lots of working class French Canadians in New Hampshire, the ones who had jobs in the mills before they started closing.

You've probably got a bloc of good, practicing Catholics there who think Johnny's family problems are a disgrace. But maybe a lot of them know from experience that family life with no money coming in can be pretty grim, even break up a home. Maybe there'd be an edge of sympathy there somewhere, something that tears them between disapproval and understanding. They're undecided about Johnny. Now remember that these are all good union people who hate those nonunion mills down south for stealing their jobs. So, maybe we could tip them into Johnny's camp by emphasizing his support for strong labor unions. Johnny doesn't have to say a thing he doesn't believe in, but he'd know when to come on strong, and with whom, to tip the balance with the undecideds. You get me? You know what I'm saying?"

"Yeah," Eileen said, radiating boredom, "okay. Now what about this salience?"

"That's research talk for does it matter a damn. Like if you asked shipyard workers on the coast here in Portsmouth if they thought private companies should be prevented from digging coal on public lands in the West, maybe a lot of them would say sure, keep 'em off the public lands. I don't know. But if you probed a little you might find that it wasn't very important to them, and Johnny's position on the issue wouldn't lose him any votes and wouldn't gain him any votes either. Simply not salient to a shipyard worker in the East, western coal isn't.

"That's it," I wound up. "That's what I want to do. Three things: Get as much as I can on where New Hampshire stands, get a feel for which issues really matter to the locals, and find out how to zero in on the ones who could go one way or the other on election day. End of course in political polling. Now you know as much as Gallup." I didn't add that if they could learn how to predict with any sort of accuracy which people would actually get out and vote on a cold November election day they'd know more than Gallup; in this trade we don't advertise our ignorance, just like any other line of business.

"All right," Delaney said. "That's enough. I get it, but I have no faith in it. Next time I think I'll cut class."

"I guess," Eileen said in a tired voice, "it doesn't hurt to try, but if you want the truth, I'm with Al. It's not going to get us anywhere." She drew a deep breath.

Delaney nodded his agreement. "Pissing into the wind, that's all we're doing."

"Okay," Eileen said in a firmer voice, "Dad said he'd go ahead, so let's get to it. After he's gone over these questions of yours, then what?"

"I polish the thing up and get together with the Daitches. They work out the computer angles, and tomorrow night we go into action with the survey."

She nodded; Delaney didn't even do that much.

The candidate announced from across the room that he was ready. He handed my material back to me, each question marked according to its urgency. "Here it is, Ev, for what it's worth, which, I'm sorry to say, isn't very much at this point. Not that I don't appreciate your wanting to try. It's a hell of a job you're taking on."

I took the papers. "Thanks, Johnny. And thanks to you all. A more touching unanimity of sentiment would be difficult to imagine."

Something between a laugh, a snort, and a gaseous eructation escaped from Al Delaney's ample gorge. "You want the truth, you're the best politician here. The rest of us say we're licked, and you say maybe, but not yet."

"Al's right," McGrath added. "Too much at stake not to give it a whirl. Too many people busting their butts for me to turn tail now. Let's do it. Let's do it right. You go to it, boy!" He clapped me on the back, both encouraging me and propelling me out the door.

I marched forward, the sound of bugles in my ears, flags flapping in my mind. A soldier boy off to war, the poor sap, the cheers echoing in his head long after the crowds have dispersed and found their ways back to their roast beef dinners and warm feather beds.

That evening the Daitches and I got together to work out the details. After that I trundled off to bed. Betty gave me some fashionable variety of pill to make me sleep, but it didn't do much for my dreams, one of which had me a respondent in a survey being conducted by the Spanish Inquisition. All my answers were wrong.

FIFTEEN

The survey went like a dream too, but a good one. The kids knew the job was important, and they put on the steam. Barbara Jellthrop was the only one who let us down. She never showed up, but the rest of us took turns filling in. Nobody stopped to yawn, and if anyone looked to be flagging, Betty or Eileen or Bill was on hand with tea, coffee, and Cokes. Everyone pitched in except for Al and the candidate himself, both off mending fences, and boy George, who was probably off mending his face, not that a mended face would have been any more of an aesthetic triumph than the busted-up version.

At this stage in the likely decline and fall of Johnny McGrath there wasn't much point in worrying whether the citizenry was going to be ticked off by being knocked out of bed for a nighttime interview, so I kept the crew going until eleven, which is definitely against the rules in the survey game. Some people slammed their receivers down, but I wanted as many interviews as we could get: If it became important for Johnny to know how blue-eyed Latinos fluent in Polish felt about the devaluation of the South African rand, I didn't want to have to say that I hadn't interviewed enough members of this key target group.

When it was over I locked the door to the Lizard Lounge with a shudder for what I sincerely hoped was the last time, and I took the whole gang up to the bar for a nightcap. I figured I'd charge it all to Puppy Luv, a new diet supplement for prepubescent doggies the agency was testing. (It was "scientifically formulated with miracle ingredient D-39X" to grow strong bones and at the same time deodorize the effluent mishaps of as yet unhousebroken pets.) We partied until somewhere between 1:30 and 2, when I had spent enough Puppy Luv research money to conduct a taste test for Weimaraners on the moon. Without me to foot the bill, the kiddies dissolved like ice cream cones in July, off to celebrate elsewhere, while oldsters over twenty-five hobbled uncertainly away to their respective pads.

Too keyed up for sleep, I flopped into a chair in my room and twiddled the TV dial. All channels were showing holding patterns except one that winked an electronic eye and advised me to insert the appropriate coinage into the attached slot so I could sneak a peek at a dirty movie. I declined, apologetically. The bedside radio was incorrectly alleged to permit access to three channels—pop, rock, and old favorites. Two were out of order. The third made noises like a cement mixer with the microphones set too close to the action. Standard motel amenities.

Crawling into bed in order to not sleep was pointless, so I descended once more to the lounge, unlocked the door, and entered. I turned on the equipment, inserted the appropriate program, flipped the switch on the printer, and waited. I waited while all my lovely tabulated results spilled out onto sheets that fell giddily into neat accordion folds. When it was complete, I tore off the last sheet, turned off the monsters, and removed the program. I locked up again and headed upstairs with the printed results, intending to snuggle into an armchair and look at what all our hard work had produced.

That did it: My eyelids slammed down and resisted re-hoisting. My trouble is that I like to figure out how to do the job, to plan it, direct it, push the buttons that make it go, but once those endless pages of numbers show up and ask to be looked at—well, I'd rather be growing apples. Figuring out sneaky ways to find out if people really dislike Johnny McGrath's dirty habits or are only jealous of them is fun, but looking at the percentages approving very much, fairly much, only a little, or not at all of this here peccadillo as compared to that there one is plain boring. I was out cold even before my bare toes had warmed the arctic zone at the foot of the bed. There's nothing like the prospect of honest labor to catapult even a postgraduate insomniac into deep sleep.

Sometime during the night bells went off. I tucked them tidily into a dream and snuggled further into my own warmth, like a cat curling up on itself. The sound persisted and when an acrid smell like a New Jersey refinery was added to the mix, the dream was cracked. I was out of bed in a flash. I did what you're not supposed to do; I dressed before I ran out, because—and my mother would have been proud—I didn't want anybody to see me in torn pajamas, fire or no fire.

A loudspeaker voice that dripped with cool and calm urged everyone into the lobby with all due dispatch. I milled around with the crowd until I recognized Betty Gold from behind, which, despite her shapeless robe, wasn't much of a trick, given the lady's Rubenesque quarters. "Betty! What's going on, you know?"

"Somebody said there's a fire downstairs, but not a big

one. Hey, they always say it's not big, don't they? You think we should get our tails out of here before two hundred people hit that front door at the same time?" Her rising voice joined in song with the wail of approaching sirens.

"No." I tried to calm her down. "Never run away this close to pay day. Anyway, it's too cold outside. Let's just get near the door and see what happens next. Any of the others around?"

"McGrath was here a couple of minutes ago, but Al found him a sack with some local pol and the two of them beat it. Eileen's in the lobby, and I think that's Bill over there in the silk paisley, and—oh, hell, look for yourself. I don't know where I am myself."

The kitchen wheeled out several coffee wagons, and as the mob regrouped around them I spotted George. He was sporting bunny-patterned jammies under a tatty terry robe, and he was all by himself—who would risk being discovered in a smoldering ruin anywhere near George McGrath? The boy was trying to look self-contained and indifferent, and in the excitement I very nearly felt sorry for him.

"Ladies and gentlemen, may I have your attention, please," a speaker system requested. A crescendo of shushes rose to epic proportions, but gradually subsided, notwithstanding the inevitable three or four persistent yammerers. "There has been a minor trash basket fire in one of the downstairs rooms. There have been no injuries, and our fine Manchester fire department tells us that the blaze is now completely under control." A series of crashes rose up the central stairwell, either to emphasize or give the lie to the proclamation. "However, you are requested not to return to your rooms until the smoke has cleared and the firemen are certain there are no remaining embers. Chairs and tables are being set up in the Daniel Webster ballroom on the mezzanine level for those of you who cannot find not find seats in the lobby, and the kitchen is preparing more coffee and pastries for those who wish it. We regret the inconvenience, and we thank you for your cooperation."

The crowd thinned as some people trudged up a flight to the elegant confines of the Daniel Webster ballroom (tufted pink leatherette walls to chest height, with occasional tuftings undone, oldie timie wallpaper (ladies with parasols) equally suitable for the motel chain's southern units, and chandeliers with glow filtering seductively through dusty glass prisms). I saw the Daitches seeking shelter 'neath the spreading branches of a plastic palm, his arm around her, her head on his shoulder. They couldn't have looked more forlorn if they had been cast out into the snow.

With Betty on my arm we headed toward the waiflike creatures. Bill Toscani and Eileen McGrath arrived at the same time. "Come on, you two kids," Betty coaxed. "Cheer up. It's all over now. Life can't be all that bad."

Two sad-eyed baby faces looked up. "You want to bet?" one asked. "That fire. It was no trash basket. And it was set."

The other explained further. "In the lounge. All our equipment. All the work. Smashed, burned. Waterlogged, if nothing else."

"Ruined," the first one concluded, as they drew even closer together.

"Oh, gosh," Betty sympathized. "That's awful. I'm so sorry."

"You're insured, I guess," I volunteered, not being able to think of anything more comforting to say.

"We're covered," Josh said, "but that's not the point."

"Somebody's doing this. Deliberately!" Ginny burst out. "That's what's so spooky. It's so senseless it makes me sick. Sick and scared." She shuddered.

There was nothing anyone could say. So I said it. "Now look, for what it's worth, none of this is directed at you two. Somebody's out to gum up the works for Johnny McGrath, and you simply happen to be part of the works. There's nothing for you personally to be worried about. At least there's that," I concluded lamely. "I guess."

"Yeah," Betty observed. "Speaking of your imitation silver linings."

One of us laughed. I forget who. We all started laughing. At least I thought it was laughing that we were doing, but as I look back on it, I'm not completely sure.

SIXTEEN

Back in my room again, I knew there wasn't going to be any more sleep. And I knew that the approach of daylight wasn't going to bring the uninterrupted quiet I needed to go over the survey findings. Back on Madison Avenue the agency kept a hotel suite permanently available for people to hole up in when they needed to think in peace, free and clear of telephones, subordinates requesting instructions, and superiors issuing them. But Manhattan was a shade too far from Manchester for practical consideration.

    The weekend place Jane and I had in Woodstock in apple country north of Manhattan was far off too, but not as far as the city. Why not, I asked myself. If I got in the car, headed south to 495, hit the Massachusetts Turnpike over to the New York Thruway and got off at Kingston, I could be in Woodstock with time to work a little even before lunch, and with scarcely a traffic light between here and there. I could stop for coffee on the road and incidentally call Jane and ask her to come up too. The two of us together could milk this survey stuff of whatever there was to find in it.

And of course I'd get to see her, which might have been the most important reason of all to hop down. The more I thought about it the more it sounded like a good way to get the work done, refresh my jaded spirits, and still be back by nightfall of the next day. My conscience wondered briefly whether I would be going off so I could work better or goofing off so I could see Jane. Then I decided I would be doing it for my employer if I checked out of the motel and saved one night's room charges. After I dreamed that one up I thought about it some more, for maybe four seconds, before I grabbed the tabulations, shoved a change of clothes into my briefcase, scribbled a note for Al Delaney to let him know I was taking the survey materials to Woodstock, carted my bag to the motel's storage room, checked out at the front desk, and made another reservation for the next day. I walked to the front door and then wheeled back again to leave the note for Delaney at the desk. Then I was all set for the road.

As I threw my briefcase into the trunk of the car I saw George McGrath in front with his own packed bags. He was hanging on to the courtesy phone that would bring the airport limo. He must have gone back to his room when the all clear was given, just as I had, and packed up. I hoped his bill was paid, not for his sake, but for the candidate's. He had come to Manchester to help his father, or so we all believed, but as it had developed, he would certainly achieve that goal much more effectively by getting the hell out of town and hiding somewhere.

Curiously, the man who had lifted George's change in the bar was there too, with a restraining hand planted on the boy's arm. I stood on the far side of my car, made busywork movements, and watched out of the side of my face. Neither man seemed completely at peace with the world; this was far from a fond farewell. As the airport limo drew into the driveway George threw off what appeared to be an urgent invitation to tarry yet a while. He also drew an envelope from his breast pocket and handed it over, together with a few sharp words I was fortunate enough not to be privileged to hear. Then he boarded the transport.

I watched the vehicle turn into the highway and drive off. Nothing that good had happened for John McGrath's candidacy in weeks. Maybe a tastefully staged plane crash would be even better, I mused wistfully, though I doubted that the kid would ever help his old dad quite that much, the younger generation being as selfish as it is these days. And while thinking of George's efforts to date on his father's behalf, I wondered what he had passed over in that envelope. Could George have been buying trouble for his father? Could he have been paying for services already rendered?

George's buddy went back inside, hurling a final look of contempt at the limo. I straightened up from my fussing and started for Woodstock and, I hoped, Jane, plus a day and a half of contentment. After I reached the Thruway south of Albany I pulled over to a rest stop, picked up a container of coffee, and called home; Jane would be just about half dressed by then, getting ready for a day in the office. "No, there's nothing wrong," I explained in answer to her question. "I simply had to get away and go over this junk in peace. Besides, I got downwind of the turkey hash in the coffee shop and figured I could stand a breath of apple blossoms."

"Which are three months off."

"I can dream. Anyway, why don't you drive up this morning? Take the day off and we can spend some time together. If we need a business reason, I could use your help looking over the tabulations. I really could. No bull. How about it?"

"Sure. Why not. If I can get someone to look after Billy. If I can work something out, I'll make Woodstock noonish, probably. Then tomorrow we split again in the afternoon?"

"Right. Wonderful. I'll be waiting." I sailed along, wheels scarcely touching the highway, radio off so I could sing without interference. It was still cold, it was still February, the ground was still white where it hadn't gone dingy gray, but the sun was bright. It was a time to find it startling once again, as if it had never happened before, that the days were getting longer and the sun was getting higher, and that the frozen earth would soon come out of its trance and get busy manufacturing apples green, apples red, and even apples yellow.

Once in the cottage I settled down for a work session, after which I found a can of tuna for lunch, mixed it with an elderly stick of celery and some mayo, and popped it in the refrigerator to wait for Jane's arrival. I did a little more work and finally stretched out with a pad and a pencil on the daybed we use for a combination sofa and guest sack. Thus primed to commit a few world-shaking profundities to paper, I promptly fell asleep, still clutching the pencil in my chubby little fingers.

When I awoke I found Jane standing over me, her hand on my shoulder. "Passed out over his work again, dead to the world. Oh, Mr. Franklin, I'd know you anywhere. You've been giving too much of yourself, driving yourself too hard. Again."

"Hi," I said blearily. "Yeah, it's me. Whatsisname." She sat on the edge of the daybed. "It's so damn good to see you. I hate being away like this." I ran my hand up her arm and behind her neck and pulled her toward me.

She stiffened. "Uh, don't you want to say hello to Billy, dear?"

I focused over Jane's shoulder and saw my thirteen-year-old stepson. He was looking at me cynically, the amused but kindly contempt of a new generation for the arthritic fumblings of the geriatric set writ large on his young face. "Hello to Billy," I said with patently false nonchalance. "How's it, son?" A thought struck me. "Hey, shouldn't you be in school?"

Jane flew to the defense of her nestling. "He's getting a cold so I kept him home. And tomorrow's just a museum trip anyway. You can take him on that when we all get back. He's promised to stay inside by the fire, and I thought it wouldn't hurt." Jane was babbling, a little too much explanation, a little defensive, which wasn't at all like her. She turned to the boy. "Feeling all right after the trip, Billy?"

"Oh, Ma, I'm okay," he answered, plainly suffering from nothing beyond a desire to stay out of school and get to the cottage, plus an overdose of parental concern. "And how you, Ev?" he asked me. I half expected him to add, "Ya gettin' much up there in Manchester?" but he kept his adolescent yawp clamped shut.

"I'm fine, Billy. I'm only sorry your mother and I have work to do before I split again for Manchester. Which reminds me: Jane, why don't you and Billy get yourselves set while I get the tuna salad out of the box. Then I'd like to show you some of this garbage I brought down and see what you can make of it."

Billy built a fire and snuggled in with a book, while Jane and I settled down over the political tabulations. For an eminently satisfying stretch of time there were no sounds beyond the crackling of logs, the turning of pages, and some quiet discussion about the significance of 60 percent in favor of one thing versus 49 percent opposed to something else. Gradually the afternoon segued from books and tabulations into hors d'oeuvres, and the coffee cups, vaguely rinsed, became cocktail glasses. Actually, my cocktail container was a cracked Royal Doulton teacup with a floral pattern, because I have always believed a martini in a cracked teacup with a floral pattern to constitute the most delicious debauchery a middle-class mentality like mine can endure.

The steak and potatoes Jane had had the foresight to pick up in town found their ways into the oven, while the Swiss chard from last year's garden thawed and bubbled in a saucepan. We folded our work and sat contentedly watching the fire and sniffing the dinner as it worked its way toward completion. The room was several degrees warmer than spoilsport conservationists insist is necessary for health, and it was wonderful.

"I wish we could live here," I said.

"Me too," Billy added.

"Stop whining, you two," Jane ordered. "I know. And we will, someday. But before everybody melts into a puddle of mellow, let's get the table set; the steak is about ready." Billy and I traded glances. Women are so hard, so practical.

The next morning was bright and clear again. Jane and I finished our work, and we settled back to relax. Billy's cold was miraculously cured, and he went down to the village to see what kind of trouble he could rustle up. We curled up by the fire again, Jane and I, after carefully locking the front door. This time when I put my hand behind her neck there was no need to observe the social amenities such as saying hello to Billy or to anybody else except, of course, to Jane herself, my long lost wife. Me Tarzan, Jane Jane.

SEVENTEEN

Midmorning, we parted again. Billy would be dropped off at school for the afternoon session, after the museum trip, and Jane would head for the office. I started out for Manchester feeling refreshed and alive and up to facing what I hoped would be my last few days as a political pundit. I'd hand over my results and then, never looking back, I'd sail into the mists until I reached the shores of, if not the Elysian fields, at least Manhattan.

On the road I kept turning over what Jane and I had dug out of the data for presentation to the candidate. I had a few far-out suggestions to which I knew he would object, but I also had the facts and figures to back myself up. Both McGrath and Delaney were reasonably quick studies, and I was comfortable with the notion that they might go along with me once they saw what the survey showed.

The survey! I suddenly realized that the briefcase full of facts and figures was still in Woodstock. I had put it in my briefcase along with my pajamas and toilet articles and then up and left without it. Since I was already on the Massachusetts Turnpike there was no point in turning back. If Johnny listened to me but needed further convincing I could drive down and back again in half a day, with maybe Bill Toscani along to help at the wheel.

That's not the way it worked. In the motel parking lot I flew out of the car and into the eagerly waiting arms of George McGrath's two unsavory drinking companions. "Hold it, sweetheart," the lead one said. "Just you hold it there. About time you got here, damn it." He twisted my arm up behind my back. "That's for making me wait the whole goddamn day. You like it?"

"What the hell is this! Let me go!"

"Sure, sure. You hand over them whatzit survey things and you get your arm back. One for one. Nobody gets hurt. Get it?"

"No. Screw you. Cut it out. Let me go!"

"Ah, gee, Joey, he says no. Whadda we gonna do, he don't wanna play nice." My arm went up my back an extra inch. "I think you're gonna turn it over, so do it now, nice and quiet. Don't get hurt. I wouldn't wanna hurt a good boy like you, would I, Joey?"

Joey shook his head from side to side, but his ears failed to flap like a spaniel's.

I gasped. "Besides, I don't have them. I forgot to pick them up. I mean it, you two!"

"Look in his car," my captor said to the other one. "Dump whatever he's got in there and look for a pisspot of papers with numbers on them. And check the trunk." To me he said, "Think ya fuckin' funny, hey? We'll see about that."

The second one did as ordered and came back empty-handed, shrugging his shoulders to indicate failure.

I felt a new pressure in the ribs. "You know what this is, Franklin? It's black and shiny and it goes boom if you squeeze it. Maybe you saw the movie." His head was close to my ear; anyone passing would think we were having a confidential discussion. I smelled garlic, yesterday's garlic. "You want I should squeeze it?"

"Look," I said, "I'm not kidding, for Christ's sake. I forgot the damn things when I packed. They're over in New York, God's truth."

"Don't shit me, you—"

The other one intervened cautiously. "Hold on, Pete," he said. "Not here. Anyway, maybe he's telling the truth. I think maybe you oughta check the car too. You don't find nothing either, we take him to Boston. We do that, the boss'll find out what's going on."

"I dunno about that." Clearly the junior partner's venturing an opinion wasn't protocol. "Well, awright. You watch the baby." He gave my arm a vicious twist, ground his heel into my foot, and strode off.

I winced and gasped. "Listen," Junior said, "you gotta understand. Pete's in a bad mood; his kid got left back last term. Flunked his goddamn English, something like that."

I couldn't imagine why, I told myself, spinning dizzily between disbelief and fear. What was I, a teacher substitute? "Look, I meant it. The stuff you're after is in New York, in Woodstock!"

"Yeah, yeah, look, I believe you. Just don't get Petey any more upset, for your own good. Keep your mouth closed."

The disillusioned father came back. "We're gonna go to Boston," he announced grimly. "Better not get so smart with the boss, Franklin, you like to keep your ass together. Joe here is gonna let go your arm and you walk nice and quiet to that green Olds over there." He jutted a stubbly chin into the air. "Get between us, and don't try nothing. Now move."

I moved, rigid as a wooden soldier, but I moved. They

put me in the place of honor next to the driver's seat. The head one drove. We proceeded in total silence, the smooth hum of the car providing the constant backdrop for my disjointed thoughts. At one point the driver said, "This punk is making us look stupid. Boss ain't gonna like it, I tell ya." The other one grunted. We went on in silence again.

Ten minutes later he repeated, "Stupid, that's what," but to himself. The other one didn't answer.

We pulled into a wooded rest stop. No other cars were parked. "You know what I'm thinking, Joey?" the driver asked.

"Aw, come on, Pete. He didn't do nothing. Leave the guy alone."

"He did enough."

"Boss ain't gonna like it, you mark him up."

"Boss'll never know. Go ahead." There was no movement. "Joey, I'm telling ya. Go ahead!"

"Ah, shit." From the back seat Joey grabbed me by the hair and pulled my head back. The one next to me hurled himself out of his own seat and over me, slapping my face back and forth. "That's fuh doing nothing, punk." He swatted me harder; I tasted blood. "And that's fuh making me look stupid." My head swiveled from side to side. "And here's one to grow on, shithead," he announced as he slammed me in the gut.

Either the restricted space in the car or his fear of the boss kept him from getting up enough steam to hurt me badly. No teeth were loose, but I could taste bile, and my stomach felt like death. I had no choice but to keep my mouth shut, no strength to do anything else even if I had been stupid enough for a macho gesture, but I promised myself that if I got out of this in one piece, somehow I'd pay my friend Petey back, make him wish he'd beaten up his wayward son instead, if he hadn't already done so. It might have to be done in my wimpy, white-collar way, it might not involve physical hurt, though I hoped it did, but it was going to happen. I was going to pay him back.

We reached Boston. Driving through streets that had never heard of Beacon Hill, the car stopped in front of a bar neoned in red as The French Connection. I was ushered in between my two escorts through the kitchen and up one flight. A door at the end of the hall led into a room that filled the entire width of the building. I looked at it almost in shock, as if some delirium had set in. The space was almost too grand to be called an office, though that was what it most resembled. Several deep oriental rugs were scattered around the floor, the largest and most central being a Kirman, which if it isn't the most costly of all is close enough to make no difference to you and me. There were large overstuffed chairs and an outsize camelback couch. All was brocade, green and red and gold thread. Lots of gold thread. No sleek and modish veneers, no rosewood, teak, or walnut disgraced the monumental desk or the occasional tables; all was burning, deep red mahogany, so far out it was beyond style. Next to this, Ed Jorgensen's office, assembled by many fashionable decorators at stockholders' expense, looked like the shack in a parking lot.

In an alcove that must have once been a separate room, practically in the middle distance, the effect became incongruous. Arrayed were a gymnasium mat, rowing equipment, a stationary bicycle, weights, and several gadgets that looked as if they had been invented solely for the purpose of separating narcissistic yuppies from their overburdened bank balances. The bicycle was occupied by a man of at least seventy sporting a full head of gleaming silver hair pompadoured and ducktailed into a tender reminiscence of prime Elvis Presley, a barrel chest, more muscles than I had seen since enforced gym classes in high school, and a salt and pepper moustache of British colonel magnificence.

The two hoods announced me, though with somewhat

less formality than the sumptuous setting deserved. "This here's Franklin, boss. We hadda bring him in. He's holding out on that crap you wanted."

Boss waved them out impatiently. "Good. You boys wait outside. Sit down, Mr. Franklin. I'll be eight minutes more," he promised after consulting his Rolex. "Have to keep to my exercise schedule."

I considered my options. Then I sat. Eight minutes later an alarm tinkled a phrase from Mozart's Fortieth. My host grabbed a towel, mopped himself off, donned a terry robe, and started walking rapidly around the room. "Can't stop now," he said. "Cool down. Why, I don't know, but it's called for. So they say, anyway."

Finally he flung himself into a chair and faced me. "Well. At last. Let me introduce myself. Pierre LeGrand."

I had heard the name. Then I remembered. The man who set the odds that went against Johnny McGrath, the man whose name was always mentioned along with those words that trip freely off everybody's lips but that nobody understands—syndicate, boss of the New England territory, capo dei capi.

It showed in my face, and that pleased the man. "Ah, you know of me. I apologize for your finding me like this, for making you wait. I exercise. My doctor." He raised his hands in mock helplessness; his nails were polished. "It reduces cholesterol, whatever this cholesterol is. If the witch doctors know themselves. My son, fifty years old and still a smart aleck, he's very American—I'm still French Canadian, a Canuck, square—he says it stops the arteries from hardening in the brain, you know? Looks at me on these machines, says I'm a charter member of the Three S Club. You know what this is?"

I shook my head, as much to rid myself of a dizzy feeling as to answer in the negative. I'm not sure I could have spoken, anyway. He went on. "Three S. Seniors for a Sane Senility. The little bastard. But I ramble. I'm sure you'd like to get back to Manchester, isn't that right?" He didn't wait for my answer. "Have a cigar. Cuban. You'll like it. Take two, Mr. Franklin. Take as many as you like."

I took two, which was really two more than I liked. I don't know why; maybe I interpreted the invitation as a kind of order. I lit one, playing for time, trying wildly to understand what was happening to me.

"You like it?" my host inquired.

"Yes, as a matter of fa—" I coughed horribly.

"Here. Drink this." LeGrand poured some water from a carafe on his desk. At least I hoped it was water. He watched me conquer the cigar smoke and he beamed. "I like you, Mr. Franklin. I like to see a man enjoy a good cigar. Personally, I'm not allowed these days, but I do it once in a while anyway. So!" He slapped his palms down on his lap. "I'll have the boys take you back to Manchester. All I want first is this survey you've got. The boys tell me you wouldn't hand it over." He shook his head. "Very foolish." He waggled a finger at a stubborn child.

"But I told them. I didn't have it. I don't have it."

LeGrand sighed. "Mr. Franklin. I don't know what this is, these percentages here, percentages there, that makes it so important. I'm a simple business man. What I do know is that I've got a lot of money riding on this election. My sources tell me you have something that could maybe help the wrong man win. Maybe, maybe not. Nothing personal, but to be honest, I don't believe it. But I can't take no chances. Any chances, I mean. Half a century speaking English, I still make mistakes. To make it simple, you could get hurt." He nodded for emphasis. "You really could get hurt. Even your family, they could get a little bit hurt."

"Listen, Mr. LeGrand, those two goons wouldn't listen to me. They were too busy collecting money from George McGrath for all this dirty work that's been going on. But I told them the truth. I didn't have the survey with me then; I don't have it with me now."

"I don't know anything about George McGrath, except he's a useful fool, a fall guy. But small potatoes, eh? I'm a major entrepreneur, Mr. Franklin, and I don't sell retail. No George McGraths." He laughed, immoderately amused by his own wit. "No retail, get it? And I think you're trying to shift us from the main point. To get back, what did you say to my boys? Tell me. I listen better. The boys are reliable as far as it goes, but not too bright. Tell, tell." He urged me on, flapping his fingers from me toward himself.

"It's this way. You knew I had taken the survey down to my place in Woodstock. I don't know how you knew that, but you did. Okay. I worked on it down there for a day and then I came back. But I forgot the stuff! I simply left it there. Why would I lie, with those two, two—"

"Hoodlums?"

"—hoodlums holding a gun on me? Look, I've got the key to the place, and they can pick it up there. I'll give them directions. Only please, no trouble. Leave my family out of this."

"Oh, now you hurt me. Please! This isn't pennies, but on the other hand it's not something Pierre LeGrand would do anything serious about. A broken arm, maybe. A leg in a cast for a month or two, but what the hell, young boys, they heal fast. So don't worry so much. But if you're telling it straight, this foolish survey is in your cottage, well, like the kids say, no sweat. That'll be the end to it. I give you my word!"

"That's the truth. There's no survey worth that much trouble, so take it and welcome. I don't see where it's going to do you much good, but take it. Only leave my family out."

He laughed again, a regular jolly old St. Nick. "I agree with you about what it's worth, but I take no chances, oui? Again, don't worry. It's a pleasure to do business with you. And if it eases your mind, I should tell you that I'm staying out of unnecessary unpleasantness these days because I plan to return to Quebec very soon, and I don't need trouble to get in the way. It's funny, I did very well here in the States, but never once did I feel at home. Here, they all say my Christian name like they were saying how it smells in a men's room. On the other hand, when I was a kid back home, us back-country French never had two bits to get inside a men's room and find out for ourselves what it smells like. What can I tell you? So I've made it here, my wife and I are getting on, we're going back home and be big shots. Maybe I endow a men's room up there. The Pierre LeGrand men's room, no Anglos allowed. One for the ladies too, all this fem lib nonsense.

"You know why I keep you here, why I talk away like this?" He looked at me, amused once again at my discomfort. "No, of course not. How could you? I like talking to an educated man. Pete, Joey, the others," he said, making a gesture of mock despair, "—what are they? Two footed animals. They don't talk, they grunt. Listen to me: Back home, when I was a kid, and maybe you find this hard to believe, I put myself through college at night. In Quebec." He shook his head for emphasis, and put up a hand as if to stop me. "Yes, I did, Mr. Franklin. No, I admit, I didn't get my degree, I didn't finish, but I nearly got there. Business administration. I had some fool idea I'd open a restaurant, until I found out—in those days things were very different for anybody named LeGrand, even in Quebec—I found out that in a restaurant the LeGrands were the bus boys, maybe at most a maître d'hotel, but the owner was Mr. Smith or Mr. Jones, or the banks didn't make the loan. That was the way the English God wanted it." He laughed. "So I dropped the idea of a degree, and changed my line of work for something more suitable for a Canuck. It's worked out well, as you can see," he assured me, his arm making a sweep of the room. "Another cigar?"

I declined. "Thanks. What I'd really like is to get back to

Manchester, but I haven't got a car. Your boys left mine behind."

"Ah, I apologize for them. They can't think ahead. The help you get these days for reasonable money is nothing but *tsouris,* as my Italian business associates would put it. I tell you what: To make up for your inconvenience, I'll have one of them drive you back in my car. And I'm sure I don't have to remind you that if we don't find this survey of yours where you say we will, it would be wise of you to remain in Manchester until we can talk to you again. *Soyez sage,* as my mother used to advise me. I've enjoyed talking to you."

He liked me; he enjoyed talking to me; he kept assuring me of that. He probably liked puppy dogs and enjoyed talking to them too, but I'd hate to have been around when he decided, with almost certain regret, that it was time to put the little fellow, as the expression goes, to sleep.

I drew a deep breath and decided to test the extent of his affection. "Mr. LeGrand," I said, "you know as much about John McGrath as he does himself. Especially the scandals in his past. How'd you find it all out? Somebody must have helped you. Who?"

He didn't laugh this time. He only chuckled; it bubbled up from his throat, something like a comment from Mount Etna. "You mustn't ask me to betray a business confidence. It's bad manners, Mr. Franklin. I've got my sources, obviously."

"George McGrath, isn't it?"

He opted against a second chuckle. "I think you are going to leave now, go back to Manchester." He pushed a buzzer.

"Okay," I said hastily, "but let me ask one last thing. If you can't tell me, you can't tell me, and that'll be it. But will you let me ask?"

He nodded sternly, a judge waiting for the guilty man's last words before he pronounces sentence.

"Can you at least tell me how the word was spread around so—so efficiently? Every story about McGrath seemed to work its way across the state like a big echo, bouncing off Maine, Vermont, and Massachusetts, and then back again. How did you manage?"

He relaxed and smiled again. "Ah, that. That I can talk about, to some extent, anyway. It involves only my own organization and can't compromise any of my associates. I'm happy to tell you. Not, you understand, in detail, but enough. Suppose," he said, "somebody visits a young lady who works for me. Perhaps she has heard some rumors, and like a silly girl, she loves to gossip? I don't know, but maybe. Maybe she chatters away like a little magpie. And there's maybe a bartender where I've got some—" His hands described a few circles in the air as he searched for the words. "—business connections likes to shoot the breeze with the customers at the bar, give them the inside dope. It could be, no? And if I had any of the demimonde working for me, bookies, gamblers, which you understand I don't say I have, these, unlike you and me, are unsavory types who make their living, flourish even, on rumors, on ugly stories. Mud spreads, Mr. Franklin. Mud smears. You give it the lightest touch and it flows like lava from the bowels of the earth. Now, does that satisfy you, my friend?"

"Thank you. I think so. Thank you very much, Mr. LeGrand. And I wish you a happy retirement in Quebec. I hope you enjoy it." I was beginning to talk like him myself.

"I intend to." He looked over at the hoods waiting impatiently just inside the door. "Pete, take the Caddy and drive Mr. Franklin back to Manchester. No funny business; Mr. Franklin is my guest. Joe, you take these keys to Mr. Franklin's cottage. He'll give you the instructions you need, what to pick up. And Joe, don't go picking up anything else, you understand?"

"Yeah, James," I said to Pete, "and next time, see that your uniform is cleaner. There's drool on your bib."

LeGrand laughed; Pete didn't but I figured he'd be as helpless to do anything about it on the trip back as I had been on the trip down.

This time I sat in the back of the limo, where the bar was. And where Pete's fat fists weren't. All he could do, and he did it, was turn the radio on full blast to shatter my eardrums. Something with a full bank of electric guitars. I saved my sanity by dreaming happily of sentencing this ugly mother to pass his old age listening to a second-string Handel Society tenor bleat ballads about Fair Phyllis the Lovelorn Shepherdess and her rural swain. Maybe I couldn't achieve that, but I still intended to work on a way to pay this creature back.

One stretch limo later, me looking out the one-way windows and sipping on single malt scotch from the bar, I arrived at my motel. My prayers were answered: Betty and Bill were out front. I looked through them and said, "See to my luggage, you two. And then take the rest of the day off. After that you're fired."

Bill's mouth gaped.

"And shut up," I suggested as I passed over a Cuban butt. "Have a ten cent seegar, son, and give the broad a couple of puffs."

Two days later my key came back in the mail. No note. Weeks after, when I got to the cottage again, I found the survey had indeed been picked up. Nothing else had been disturbed except that the gin bottle was empty and my cracked tea cup was on the table. I sniffed it; it smelled of gin. Joey had finer sensibilities than I had credited him with.

EIGHTEEN

The first order of business was to tell Delaney what had happened to the work I took down to Woodstock. He phoned McGrath, who was in Concord, and told him he was on his own, that there'd be no help—or interference—from me. I sat in on an extension phone.

"Frankly," the candidate said, "I don't think it matters that much. Opinion polls are the center of your world, Franklin, but out here where the real people live they're only a single grain out of all the bits and pieces that get thrown into the hopper. A piccolo in a band of trombones and cymbals. Doesn't matter."

"I know pretty much what it showed," I said. "I can't give you the figures, but I can tell you where they were pointing. How about it?"

"I'll be back in Manchester late today and we'll see, but

offhand I'd say no. Let's skip the whole thing. Let's forget it and go ahead with what we've got." He sounded weary, defeated, like a terminally ill patient refusing the life support system. I couldn't blame him.

Before I left Delaney to break the news to the Daitches and their crew, I had to find something out. "Al," I asked, "who'd you mention that note to, the one I left saying I was taking the tabulations to Woodstock? Who knew I had run off a set before it all went up in smoke? Who the hell knew?"

"For Christ's sake, man," he said in disgust, "who the hell didn't know, would be easier. It was no secret, was it? I told everybody except maybe Havemeyer, Leich, and Duckworth, but only because I didn't run into them. Anybody who asked about the fire I told. I even bumped into Montano in City Hall and he asked about Johnny and I told him too. This game, you've gotta look like you're on top, nothing gets you down, you're in control, you're a goddamn son of a bitch of a winner!"

"Yeah, I guess. Wrong question."

"Bet your ass."

I met the survey crew in the Lizard Lounge. It had been cleaned up, but an acrid smell hung in the air—or maybe I imagined it. The only visible souvenir of the blaze was the feathery smoke trails high up on the wall, where they would remain until the next time the place was painted. The computer equipment was gone, some, I imagined, for salvage, and the rest to the Manchester dump after inspection by the insurance companies. So it goes.

As soon as Josh Daitch told me they were all present, I started my spiel, thanking them for their hard work and telling them how much it meant. I told them frankly that Johnny McGrath might not do as well as he deserved to do because somebody with a lot of money, dirty money plus talent to match, had crippled the campaign with a filthy countercurrent of lies, innuendoes, and half-truths. Then, fervently relieved that none of my Madison Avenue fellow cynics could hear, I told them that there was still a victory and that it belonged to them, and nobody could take it away. They had worked hard for what they believed in, and if it were only the predators and the nuts and the fanatics who worked hard, then the country would be ready to be packaged into individual bite-sized portions for express delivery to the groups waiting to gobble them down. I even meant it, for God's sake!

At the conclusion we shook hands all around, and the kids left. Josh, Ginny, and I were alone in the room, steam still rising from my empassioned declaration. "And in conclusion," I said, "ohshitohdear. What a lousy shame. You two going to be all right, all that equipment gone?"

"We'll be hurting, but it'll be okay. We'll get through."

"I'm glad of that at least. The cops have any idea yet who set the blaze?"

"None. They'll never find out. No way."

"Well, it was great for a little while. And so was that gang you brought in. Hey, listen, Barbara Jellthrop wasn't here again today. She still off with her boyfriend, this long?"

"I don't think so. Somebody said he's back at his job. Maybe she finally went home to see her folks."

"You think we should check?" I asked. "See that nothing's happened? I mean, what the hell, with all that's been going on."

Josh and I found the boyfriend at work in a garage across town. He wiped his hands on his coveralls when we introduced ourselves, and grinned. Another clear-eyed kid reminding me I was twenty years closer to the grave than he was. "Pleased to meet you," he said, sticking a hand out. A cloud crossed his face. "You Barbara's dad?"

Oh, all right, shut up: Maybe twenty-five years closer to the grave. I didn't say that I was her little brother, but I wanted to. Instead, I told the lad, "No, but Barbara's been working with us on the McGrath campaign. You probably know about that. We haven't seen her since before the weekend. You know where she is?"

"Gee, I thought she was with you guys. We got back too late Monday night for that survey thing, but that's when we pulled in, all right."

"What time did you get here?" Daitch asked.

"You drop her at the motel?" I put in simultaneously.

"About maybe two in the morning. Yeah, I remember it was on the car radio, a little after two. I dropped her at the motel. What's wrong? Something wrong with Barbara?"

"We don't know. Probably not, but we can't locate her. Did you see her go inside?"

"Oh, sure," He looked awkward. "I said I'd come in for a while, maybe we could have a Coke in her room or something, but she said she was too tired. She was for bed as soon as she checked to see if any of your bunch was in that office you've got set up there."

Josh and I looked at each other. "Thanks, fellow," I said. "If you see Barbara tell her to get in touch with us, and we'll do the same if we see her first."

To Daitch, once we were back in the car, I said, "She could have gone downstairs just when some son of a bitch was beginning to play with matches. I think you and I are off to see the cops, that's what I think."

The police were interested. None of this young-kids-they-just-take-off-you-know-what-I-mean-so-whyn'tcha-wait-a-coupla-days. They had something for us to look at. Something unidentified, something female. Something in the morgue.

"Description fits what you've been talking about," the detective said. "Anyway, let's take a look."

We went over to the morgue. An attendant took us to a row of lockers, opened one, and wheeled the contents half way out into the room. It was our girl, Barbara Jellthrop, gray and waxy, still clear-skinned and unmarked, but without the bloom. A flower picked and hung up in an attic to dry, a crepe paper imitation coated with wax, lacking only the one miracle ingredient to make it real—life.

"Gee, what a doll," the morgue attendant said pleasantly. "I coulda used a doll like that. No offense, gentlemen."

Josh Daitch got sick, partly, I was pleased to note, onto the attendant.

Outside again, we sat with the detective and told him what we knew. Then he told us: "She froze to death. Found her just yesterday a little ways off the road ten miles out of town. Thing was, she didn't have a hat, coat, gloves, nothing. Christ! no shoes, even."

"Was she—hurt?" Josh asked.

The policeman shook his head. "Not a mark on her. She was just there, like she had gone out of the house that way. It must've been damn near zero when it happened, for God's sake! No drugs or alcohol in her system either."

"When did it happen?" I asked.

"Near as we can figure late Tuesday night."

Josh and I spoke at once. "But she came back to the motel Monday night. Her boyfriend dropped her off." "Nobody saw her during the day on Tuesday, I'll swear to that."

We talked it over, gave the police the boyfriend's name, told them what Barbara was doing with our bunch, and, I thought most important, told him we figured she got back in time to have seen someone setting a fire, someone who would have forced her to leave the motel with them. It had been late enough on Monday night so that with the slightest bit of luck there would have been very few people around to march her past. And, worst of all, we told the man how to get in touch with her parents. I felt guilty about having them find out through the police, but I was too much of a coward to volunteer my services.

We left, dazed and somehow disappointed that what we

had just told the police didn't somehow galvanize them into a frenzy of efficient activities, leading to quick arrests and charges and convictions. Somehow I knew those two hoods that worked for LeGrand were a big part of this, just as they had been a big part of the Della DeGraaf performance in Des Moines. Furthermore, I was reasonably certain, without an iota of proof, that they had burned out our operation. They were somehow responsible for this young girl's death, even if I didn't know how, and even if I couldn't fathom the meaning of her wandering around the New Hampshire countryside on a cold February night without proper clothing. I didn't know this, I couldn't fathom that, but damn it, I was going to find out.

Those two had roughed me up, humiliated me, stolen my work, and, playing by what we called girls' rules where I come from, they had pulled my hair. Somehow it was all tied together by the effort to defeat John McGrath's candidacy by playing dirty. I had seen George McGrath paying these guys, I knew Pierre LeGrand stood to make a bundle if Johnny lost big, and he had shyly told me, with pardonable pride, how well organized he was to peddle slander across the state.

Okay then, but where did I begin? What did I begin with?

I had one feeble idea. With no more survey work to do I couldn't justify prolonging my stay in New Hampshire, but I had a presentation to make in Kansas City to the producers of Puppy Luv, the vitamin-chocked goody young pets best love to throw up, and Kansas City wasn't far from some people who could tell me the truth about Johnny. Maybe if I found out which of the conflicting stories about his wife were the real ones, or if they were all lies, or, God help me, if they were all based on fact, then maybe I could decide where to go next and what to do about it. Whatever John McGrath himself might say was the truth was beside the point; he himself was, to say the least, an interested party. What I had to know was what the folks out there in what politicians love to call the heartland of America could tell me, if they would.

Young Lochinvar had come out of the west, but this time middle-aged Lochinvar was going back to the west, chins and dewlaps flapping bravely in the breeze. Well, the Middle West, anyway.

NINETEEN

I said goodbye to Johnny and Al. "There's no point in my hanging around. You've got Bill and Betty still on the job. Hell, I'm no politician, but I think you could make a virtue of not having a pollster. Why not tell the voters you fired your polling organization, that Johnny McGrath is going to give them Johnny McGrath straight, not what some puppeteer says he should give them. I can tell you one thing I pick up all the time in my commercial polls is that people are getting mighty paranoid about the idea that somebody is manipulating them, pulling them thisaway and thataway, and that polling is the tool that's being used to do it. They're starting to look over their shoulders to see who's dogging their footsteps, and wondering why."

I got carried away. "Hell, I'd even jump the others like Havemeyer and Leich for being afraid to speak their own minds before the opinion poll results are shoveled into their heads. It's exactly like on Madison Avenue: We get a product with absolutely no food value at all and we make a virtue of it, push it with the diet market, promise it's guaranteed to give the body nothing, and charge ten percent more to the poor saps who buy it. You sacked me; make a virtue of it. There's still time, Johnny, so think about it. You've got a full week to swing some votes your way, and that's a long time in this business."

McGrath raised a cynical eyebrow. "Real nice speech. I appreciate it. I'll keep it in mind." I was dismissed.

Delaney clapped me on the back. "Thanks for trying, Ev. You did a hell of a job. Maybe we'll see you again four years from now."

"I hope so. I really hope so," I said. Then I packed up, checked out, and drove off.

Back in New York I polished up the presentation Jane had put together. We had left samples of Puppy Luv with 500 puppy proprietors in four cities, and had gone back two weeks later to find out if they had bought our brand on their own, stayed with their old brand, or had done some switching around. We had asked why they did what they did. The results were set down in a way to show Puppy Luv's strengths and weakness against the competition, the likes and dislikes—both real and imagined, which is as good as real in these affairs—and what that indicated in terms of advertising directions and possible product changes. And we developed some hunches about which brands Puppy Luv would best be able to clobber and which others were most likely to give us our lumps.

Jane had, happily, found me the flakey respondent I always like to quote in my presentations to give the client a laugh, and possibly even to keep him awake for the facts and figures. This was a housewife who said she would never buy Puppy Luv, and might even sue us, because after three days on the stuff, Rover, age eight weeks, had upped and sired an enormous litter on his own momma. Personally, we at Finch, Rowan, & Hyde were sure he had brought in outside help, I would tell them, but then you never know what all those miracle ingredient additives are going to accomplish. After the show in Kansas City I went to bed for two hours, which brought me to midafternoon. Then I made two phone calls. The first got me a date for the next day at a farm not too far from where I was, just outside Excelsior Springs. The second, somewhat further, was for the day after that in St. Joseph. Neither drive would be overly long, and I estimated winding up my trip to St. Jo early enough in the day to find transportation back to New York the same afternoon. Meanwhile, with a little time to kill in Kansas City, I went to the local museum to see the oriental collection, and then, this being big beef country, found myself a lovely steak dinner; Ed Jorgensen bought me a fine burgundy to go with it. Before turning in I made notes on what I ought to cover the next day in Excelsior Springs.

My car was the tiniest, tinniest subcompact I could rent without feeling I might be endangering life and limb. It bounced vindictively over the back roads, but I had no choice; we were under orders to keep costs down. That situation, unlikely as it might have been for a world-class advertising agency, had risen like a lava dome and burst after Big Ed himself had zoomed up to a client meeting in Indiana in a snazzy Mercedes convertible. The client, seeing him screech to a halt in the parking lot and exit the car like a hyped-up teenager, had objected to what he reasonably judged to be his company's money being ladled out to maintain Jorgensen's image of himself as a slim-gilt youth. Since a client had scolded Ed, he spun about and passed it on; a memo was spewed out by his office flunking us all downscale to modest transportation, to "project a serious and responsible attitude toward our clients and their products." (Naturally, the order did not apply to Ed himself, as we found out by having our spies in accounting riffle through his expense vouchers. Absolute power, they say, corrupts absolutely, and isn't it wonderful!)

Henry Beeler's directions were careful and concise, and I found the farmhouse with no difficulty. As he had promised, a huge and rambling Victorian house came into view over the top of a rise, standing lonely down a short driveway, surrounded by patches of yellow and brown winter earth showing through the thin covering of snow. The gray brown barren trees did nothing to relieve the sense of solitude.

It was a house to have thrilled a new bride of a hundred years ago, with its rounded wooden turret, dormer windows, and gingerbread trim framing the porch. Small stained glass ovals marked the second and third floor landings. It was a house that had grown helter-skelter with its occupants, one generation adding a summer kitchen, another extending the porch around the side and screening it in, a third lifting a section of the roof with a shed dormer to make an apartment for that unmarried daughter who taught grade school down in the village. It was a house that had watched over the generations and sheltered them with a warm, protective grace. And in its silent watchfulness it cast long, sweet shadows.

A dog barked. A yellow hound appeared from under the porch, tugging at the end of a leash. A tall, thin man in his seventies came down the front steps, still fastening a down jacket, a red hunter's cap on his head. He slapped the dog gently on the flank to quiet it, and waved me in. "You Mr. Franklin? I'm Beeler, Hank Beeler. Let's get on in out of the cold."

I followed him past a pier glass mirror in the entry, with coat hooks down the sides, and past a refectory table that would have held calling cards generations ago but now served for the piles of letters, bills, and circulars that were brought in from the box on the road. A pottery umbrella stand patterned with brown and green tendrils stood next to the table. We passed along a faded runner in an oriental pattern and entered a parlor that combined oak furniture, massive, dark, and old, looking as if somebody cared, with newer reddish maple and thin-veneered birch looking as if nobody gave a damn. A portable TV set perched on an oaken sideboard, too high to be viewed comfortably from the two easy chairs grouped across the room to face it. A spindly floor lamp with a burn-spotted parchment shade and broken lacing stood between the chairs, a swivel arm allowing the light to be directed at either of the two chairs.

A green metal mesh stacking stool, the kind that generally lives on a patio, bore the remains of a lunch, some sandwich crusts and an empty coffee cup. An apple core rested on a crumpled paper napkin, and there, behind the stool and on one of the chairs, waited a small woman with the hopeful moist eyes of a hopeless lush. Paula McGrath, Mrs. Johnny.

"My daughter Paula," Hank Beeler said. "This is Mr. Franklin, Paula," he explained in the louder than necessary voice people use to speak to children and sick people in the unconscious assumption that like as not they don't understand because they're deaf. "Came all the way from New Hampshire to see you."

"I know, Poppa," the woman shyly protested. "You already told me." She held a hand out. "How are you, Mr. Franklin? Nice trip, I hope." She didn't wait for my reply, but in her nervousness went on to say, "Johnny and I used to fly around a lot. All over the state when he was mayor. Even to Denver, once. I loved it so," she said dreamily.

"Come on, now, girl," her father said gently, "that's not the story I got from you back then."

"Oh, I know, but that's different. It was different then. I was just sort of, well, sort of complaining." Her hands fluttered. She raised one to brush a wisp of hair that wasn't there off her forehead. Then she clasped them together in her lap and looked down as if to wonder whose they were and what they'd be up to next. "How's Eileen?" she asked.

"You saw my girl?"

"She's fine," I replied, "just fine."

"And the boy? He all right?"

"He's fine too. They're both fine."

There was nothing left for us to say by way of conversation, but after a moment's pause, she continued vaguely, "I was thinking I might go see Eileen in California. One of these days, anyway. Would you like some coffee? I'll put on a fresh pot." She jumped up without waiting for my reply and headed out of the room. If you were to ask me, I'd never be able to say what length women's skirts are supposed to be, but when I see them walking I know if they're wearing something that Seventh Avenue hasn't even thought of in years. That was how Paula Beeler McGrath was dressed, in a faint memory of something that was more or less in style an indefinite number of years ago.

Her father interpreted my expression. "Yeah," he said, "she got dressed up for the company. All she's got. Not much call for fancy clothes anymore."

"I see. Sorry if I seemed to be staring."

"That's okay. You want that coffee, I'll put it on in a couple of minutes. She may get to open up the percolator, but that's all. She'll take a little nip to steady her nerves, and that'll be it. Too much excitement." He shook his head. "Poor kid. She's a good girl, really, but there's something always been wrong. I dunno, maybe it's my fault, maybe her mother's. Like as not nobody's fault, though. One of those things."

"You know, Mr. Beeler—"

"Call me Hank."

"Hank. That's not the way your granddaughter sees it. To be honest, that's why I'm here. Eileen thinks her father's to blame, and with Johnny up there in the public eye, getting to be a national figure, we need to know the worst.

We've got to be ready for anything. I hope you don't take offense at my talking like this."

He shook his head. "No problem," he said. "I told you that when you called. No problem with me taking offense or with Johnny getting hurt by what's come of Paula. Fact is, it goes back further than Johnny. The girl's almost always been this way. Like a rabbit that's fine when it stays close to home, and then out in the field it sticks its nose in the air, no reason at all, gets into a panic, and goes lickety split for the burrow.

"You know more about politics, and I guess maybe somebody can turn that into something dirty, but there's nothing to it. I can promise you that, mister. Paula's been this way since she got out of high school. Fine till then, but after that she was like that bunny rabbit. Went away to school in Kansas City, business school, but she was back in a month. She hit the bottle real hard down there and they upped and threw her out. Back home she was her old self again and we thought she was done with it. Never happened before and we figured it'd never happen again. Met John McGrath at a party when he was down here to visit some family, they dated, got engaged, married, and nobody thought a thing about it. That was that.

"Then Paula had the first baby. Eileen. She couldn't cope. Too darned much for her, and she got on the liquor again. It still didn't seem so bad, or maybe we didn't know how bad it was, but after Johnny got to be mayor up home and big in politics, being Mrs. Mayor was too much, and—" He spread his hands hopelessly, palms up. "And there you are. And here she is," he added sadly. "Poor creature."

"But Eileen says—well to be honest, Eileen says it was her father fooling around outside the marriage that started it."

"Eileen says," he mocked. "Which came first, the chicken or the egg? Maybe he fooled around, I don't know and don't much care, but I can't blame him, can you? It takes two, and believe me, my daughter did her share. Heck, no, nobody can point a finger at John McGrath. I wish they could, I wish there was somebody to hold responsible for what's become of Paula, but that's not the way it goes."

There was nothing more. "Is she getting any kind of treatment?" I asked.

"Treatment," he echoed with a rueful grin. "Sure. She's had treatment. I had her to the county hospital and they stuck her with needles and gave her pills and told themselves she was responding to the treatment. That's how they put it—responding to the treatment. They were the ones responding, though—her treatment, their response. I took her to two different psychiatrists down to Kansas City, but that dragged on and on and got nowhere. So now she's back with me, back in the burrow, where she feels safe. No more trips out into the field, and except when she's upset, like by your coming over to visit—" He raised a hand. "I'm not blaming you. No offense. If it isn't you, it's some damn fool program on the television with guns and blood. Anyway, she gets by these days, more or less."

"Tell me, Hank, if you don't mind my asking, was there anybody else after Johnny, after she came back here? Another man she got close to?"

"Lord, no. She could never face anything like that again. Scared of her own shadow. Just Paula and me, Paula and her old dad."

That was what I thought the answer would be.

He changed to a brighter tone. "Now, how about that coffee? The girl will be gone up the back stairs to get away, so come out to the kitchen and we'll see about things."

I followed Hank Beeler again, this time realizing that those shoulders were hunched as if he were anticipating the worst, another vicious blow out of nowhere. We went into a huge country kitchen, one big enough to cook up a storm for a family reunion of two dozen. There was a small painted white table covered with a clear plastic tablecloth with a daffy pattern of colored flowers galloping around the border. I knew for a certainty that Paula had timidly chosen the cloth and then had been childishly delighted by her own daring. Hank Beeler waved me into one of the two chairs beside the table, the top of which I could see through the plastic had been repainted half a dozen times after bread knives had slashed into it, children had stuck it with pen knives, and the standard array of generations of minor kitchen accidents had landed on it. All a long, long, time ago.

"Yep," Beeler said, "you see that? She's got the percolator set up, but she never got to turning it on." He held a match to the old gas burner. "Wife always was after me to get one of those new electric numbers, but we never got around to it. Milk okay? Got no cream. Sugar?"

"Just black, thanks. You know, I can't understand why Eileen insists her father is to blame for what's happened to her mother."

"Just can't face the facts, would be my guess. The girl was always close to her mother, especially after the breakup. Hung onto her as if she was afraid her ma would take off and leave her too. Can't accept that her mother is just naturally, well, sick. I figure she has to blame somebody." He sighed again.

"Tell me, does Johnny keep in touch, at least? Help out, maybe?"

"Oh, heck, yes. We don't need the money, and I told him that. But he says he wouldn't feel right any other way. Makes him feel better, I reckon. Sends a check every month, regular. I stick it in a special account for Paula for after I'm gone. You know, Mr. Franklin—"

"Ev."

"Ev, that's the only bad part, not knowing what's to come of her when I'm gone. I've got so I'm scared silly half the time, not of dying, but of not being here to take care of Paula. Dying doesn't mean a damn, far's I'm concerned, but the way a man gets whittled away at day by day and a fellow doesn't know what's coming up next and you can't plan for anything—that's what gets to me.

"Heck, you get a little sore don't heal and you fret about cancer; a toothache, you worry about the teeth you got left coming out. Eyes get tired, you start thinking cataracts. And sometimes you're right." He snorted. "Sooner or later you've got to be right! Short of breath, bingo, it's your heart." He poured us both coffee in heavy mugs with a crisscross pattern around the top. "Hope you like it strong."

"Thanks. I think I know what you mean. I'm sorry."

"Oh, shucks, don't be. I don't see many folks to complain to, that's all." He laughed. "What do you people in advertising call it—captive audience? My captive audience has been dropping off pretty quick the last ten years, like they got the plague. No, don't be sorry. Lord knows I'm not, except for the girl's sake. I'll tell you one thing, though. You got something you want to do, do it now. The missus and I kept saying one day we'd take out on a trip to New Orleans, which isn't all that far from here. See it all, the French Quarter, the Garden District, a couple of famous restaurants. Had the money for it, too. She always wanted to see where the Mississippi ended up, the bayous. Then one day we looked around and it was too late. What'd we need the nightlife on Bourbon Street for, our age? And that rich food, we'd have been up all night with the bicarb.

"Well, we never did it. Now she's gone, and I couldn't do it on account of Paula, even if I wanted to. Which I don't." He cleared his throat. "Time for me to stop crying in your beer, young fellow, and get back to your problem. What else can I tell you? Or do for you?"

"Not a thing. You've told me what I needed to hear. I'm

satisfied and I thank you. I'd like to suggest, though, that you be real leery about any reporters that come out to look you up. Some of them, if they don't see a story ready made, they'll help one get invented. Put words in your mouth, no matter how careful you are. If you have any trouble and you want to talk it over, give me a call. There's a lot of people in my office who know how to deal with situations like that." I handed him my card. "Don't hesitate, now. Anytime you call I'll see how we can help."

"I gotcha. And I sure do appreciate it." He looked at my card, ran a finger over the embossed lettering, and tucked it in a shirt pocket. "Don't you worry, though. I won't let anything happen that could hurt Johnny. For Paula's sake; can't afford to let her get upset more than necessary."

"Right you are."

We talked for half an hour over another cup of coffee, and then I left, reassured but sad. As I climbed into the car something made me look up at the second story. She was sitting there, waiting for me in the window. She opened it and called, "Goodbye, mister. I forget your name. It's been a real pleasure. And, oh, would you remember to give my love to my babies? Tell them their mother thinks about them all the time."

"I sure will, Mrs. McGrath. The pleasure's mine."

She raised one of her fluttering hands in a farewell salute as I drove off. Through the side view mirror I could see her as I turned into the highway, her hand still lifted, prolonging the goodbye until I was out of sight, a hand raised as if to touch a life or a world that was out there somewhere but always just out of reach or out of sight.

TWENTY

I spent the night in Excelsior Springs, an old health spa that time had passed by or even run away from. There were water taps in the hotel lobby labeled variously for arthritis, kidney stones, and upset stomachs. The streets were liberally provided with benches for the elderly vacationers to rest on while they waited for transportation, whether in the form of public buses or hearses, and a few poor souls looked resigned to boarding whichever arrived first. The combination of the town and my visit to the Beeler farm left me filled with a regret for something I couldn't define, something to do with the passage of time, all going in one direction with no turning back for revisions.

Once on the road the next morning, my mood lifted, and as I headed toward St. Jo I turned over what I had learned. Paula McGrath, whether through nature or nurture, was a sweet, frightened, gentle drunk, and she had achieved the condition all on her own, with no help from her husband. If there was a culprit, it was life itself. Eileen's assessment of who was responsible was wrong, but understandably could be something she needed to believe. Eileen needed to see her mother as the innocent victim, and where there's a victim there's a victimizer, in this case her father. Anyway, that could be one interpretation of Eileen's flawed version of the facts.

George's story, that there was another man somewhere, an old-fashioned cad, a bounder, a trifler with a woman's affections, was pure madness, and had not the slightest relationship to the actual situation, except insofar as it took John McGrath off the hook. I couldn't even begin to develop a theory as to how George had arrived at such a complex fabrication, or why he would have bothered to detour so far from the truth.

Where precisely did this leave me? Good question; no answer. I put my foot down on the accelerator and sped away from my bewilderment. On to St. Jo and Johnny's mother, Anna McGrath. I was more confused than ever so I followed the national maxim: When in doubt, do something, anything, but do it.

In contrast to the Beeler place, the house I drove up to was a bungalow in a neat suburban development, all on one floor, a combination of tan brick and wood painted white. You could almost hear the occupant explaining, "After the children's father went I got rid of the old place. Too much for an elderly party like me to keep up," she would have said, using a merry tone that indicated that she didn't think it was too much at all. "You can't imagine how the dust used to collect in that old barn! And those stairs! Not to mention the heating bills. Got a spare room in this one too, though it doesn't look large from the outside, for when Johnny comes to visit." And you'd get the idea that Johnny came to visit as seldom as decency would permit.

I never would have guessed that Anna McGrath was Johnny's mother, but her claim to being Eileen's grandmother was incontrovertible. The resemblance was phenomenal, though a phenomenon gone a bit dry and harsh. She had the same wound-up intensity as the younger woman, a mouth compressed like a steel spring, hair waved and set against her head as if restrained for safety's sake, and round red arms habitually folded against an ample chest where they presided in judgment on anyone who hadn't scrubbed the kitchen floor with a strong disinfectant every Monday morning for fifty years whether it needed it or not.

Not that the lady was anything but hospitable. And I realized that she was the type of doughty woman who had made this country great, picking off dozens of Indians from the back of the Conestoga wagon after her husband had been mortally wounded and then seeing to the children's dinner. But that much iron in the backbone easily takes on the odor of an accusation of the rest of us. There was an air of independence to her, an unattractive air that said I will never be a burden to anyone, but said it in a way calculated, however unconsciously, to suffuse her family with guilt.

In short, Anna McGrath hit me as a woman whose aim was to be a burden to none and a pain in the ass to all.

In anticipation of my arrival the good tea service had been laid out. I could spot the empty spaces in the glass-fronted cabinet where the china cups were normally on display, tilted upward on teakwood stands, and taken down only for occasional special company.

After I had been put at ease by appropriate chitchat about Johnny and the grandchildren and the differences between the rigors of winter in Missouri and New Hampshire ("I expect it's six of one, half a dozen of the other, Mr. Franklin."), Anna McGrath formally opened the meeting: "But you don't want to waste your time gossiping about the weather with an old woman," she informed me. "You've got your schedule to keep, so tell me what you want to ask and I'll see what I can do." There was no question at all about who was chairing this affair, though Mrs. McG would have termed herself chairwoman, and no nonsense about chairperson, young fellow. Okay, it was her house, and, who knows, maybe the bridge club was due in a couple of hours.

"Good. I appreciate that. Before I start, I want to say that there's nothing wrong, nothing to get worried about. But a man in Johnny's position—well, there's always people looking for scandal, poking around for rotten spots, not because they know they're there, but because they figure it never hurts to try. Do you know what I'm saying?"

She waved a hand impatiently and placed it back across her chest in the judgment position. "Like squeezing vegetables down to the Safeway even when they look good. You don't have to explain."

"Fine. Okay." I cleared my throat and started tiptoeing onto the eggs. "The thing is, you see, somebody's trying to find some mud in Johnny's marriage, and we have to know how to deal with it when they start slinging it around. That's the whole problem put as simply, as bluntly, as I know how." She started a protest but I cut her off. "What we need is to know the facts, the plain truth, before somebody starts twisting things, so we can keep down the damage to Johnny. That's the problem—keeping the damage down. For one thing, there are two stories going around right now, and if one was true the other would have to be false. They're about Mrs. McGrath, Johnny's ex, and her drinking. If we knew what happened we'd know how to handle it. That's our first worry."

"Poor, sad, girl," Anna McGrath said in a tone that proclaimed almost as much disapproval as it did sympathy. "She wasn't up to Johnny, not really. A good girl, but really very limited. That was it in a nutshell. Born a plain country girl and the good Lord meant her to stay that way."

"I understand. But there's a rumor circulating that she started drinking while they were married and that Johnny himself was at the root of the problem—" I was picking up my words and laying them down as daintily as if they were sticks of dynamite. "—and then there's another story that she only hit the, uh, became a problem drinker, so to speak, after they broke up. When her second marriage failed to come off."

"Well, that one's easy," the lady smiled comfortably. "It was the girl's drinking broke up her marriage to Johnny."

"I was afraid you might say that. You see, that way, there could be people who'd try to make a case that your son drove his wife to drink and then abandoned her."

"Oh, pooh!" She dismissed the notion scornfully. "That girl was a drinker her whole livelong life. Don't believe me, Mr. Franklin, but you just ask her daddy and he'll tell you the same. Ask anybody down to Excelsior Springs and that's what you'll hear. Everybody knew all along, but they kept shet up when Johnny came along to propose to the girl. Peculiar sense of right and wrong some people have." She sniffed.

"But ma'am, your grandson himself told me that it was the second marriage falling through that caused the trouble, and he says you told him that. It just doesn't make sense."

"Well, I did tell him that." She looked bemused. "I did indeed. I don't tell a lie lightly, young man, but I know my Christian duty. Just between us, my son didn't know his. I told John it was his place to stick with that girl no matter what."

As Anna McGrath talked I was aware, even if she wasn't, that she spoke only of "that girl," "the poor girl," "the country girl," and never once of Paula Beeler McGrath. She was distancing herself, the way she might from a dead mouse by holding it at arm's length, its tail pinched between her thumb and forefinger as she carried it out to the trash bin.

"He saw it different," she went on, "and he left the girl. He tried, he's not a bad man, but finally he left her. He's my son, John is, but I'm the first to say he did wrong. No one's got the right to walk out on a marriage, especially when it's been blessed with children. George was only a tad of five then and he came to live with me. I can tell you that child was broken up something fierce. Yes, he was!" She thumped the arm of the chair for emphasis. "No mother, no father, just his old granny. Eileen was older, of course, and better able to keep herself in one piece. But not the boy.

"Well, maybe two years went by and he seemed all right, he looked all right, but I knew different. He had what they call a fragile ego?" She looked at me doubtfully. I nodded in understanding. "And he was hearing stories about his ma and her drinking, heaven knows from where." She shook her head in disbelief. "He came to me, and I lied, Mr. Franklin, I just plain lied. It's more important for a child to love his mother than his father. That's how I look at it, anyway, even if mebbe it is old-fashioned. But at the same time I wanted to protect his daddy too, so I said that they broke up because they only liked each other but didn't love each other anymore—which I reckon he never understood—and that afterwards some other fellow let his ma down real bad and that's when she took to drinking more than was good for her. A white lie, for the boy's sake.

"And that's the way it was. I couldn't keep George from hearing things, but I was able to twist 'em around a mite so he wouldn't blame his mother or his father either, and he wouldn't blame himself, which I guess was the most important thing. The whole thing was somebody else's fault, was the way I tried to make it look. And from what you say he believed me, and he still does. I did the right thing, mister, and you can take that from me. I know about these things, because I'm a mother, Mr. Franklin."

Indeed she was, and she brandished the condition like an accusing finger. Maybe she did do the right thing, but I had to wonder how much Anna McGrath did things because they were right and how much they were right because she did them. And I was getting even more confused than when I began this expedition, when I expected to find out, at the very least, that George McGrath was up to some kind of mischief related to his father's campaign. I knew for certain he was somehow connected to a couple of trouble-making hoods who worked for a man determined to ruin the candidate's chances. And I knew that some knowledgeable person had been feeding the rumor mill with half-truths about Johnny. But what I couldn't figure out was why George would hand over a patently false story that probably couldn't be made to stick. After all, there were some better items about his father's extramarital sorties that had more than a little truth to them.

Even if I knew the answers there'd still be the question of why he'd want to do it in the first place. After all, being Crown Prince of America came with a key to the front door to the White House. Lotsa broads, lotsa fun, lotsa everything free and easy.

Three times I opened my mouth to speak and three times I found that I didn't know what I wanted to have come out of it. The fourth time I simply gave up and said, "That about covers it, I think, unless there's anything you'd like to add." She shook her head; the oracle could have said plenty, her expression told me, but she had signed off for the day. "I have to thank you for being so frank. But," I added hesitantly, "there is just one more thing."

"Certainly." Those broad arms got themselves folded against the chest with finality, and she looked me straight in the eye.

"Do you think I might have another piece of that fruitcake before I go? I haven't tasted anything like that since I left home."

She laughed. "Why, bless you. Of course." A slab larger than the first one was hoisted onto my plate. "Only a real mother can make a cake like this, I can tell you."

That's what I figured too. She'd have baked it when she had knocked off her quota of redskins for the day. But it was damn good. And she was generous with it. Life can be very complicated.

TWENTY-ONE

My mother always figured that a growing child needed a steaming bowl of oatmeal every morning during the winter months. I hated oatmeal. ("It looks like cat puke, Ma. Do I hafta?") She would appear, devious woman that she was, to give in: "Just one more spoonful, that's all." After that, "Now another one for Dad." Then, "How about one for Grandma?" We'd run out of oatmeal before we ran out of relatives, even though it was on occasion necessary to drag in an uncle by marriage.

Forty years later and I was starting the same routine, only this time I was doing it to myself. I was half a continent from home, hating every minute of it. I had learned nothing useful, solved no puzzles, and was taking nothing back home except the memory of a gorgeous chunk of fruitcake. For all I had accomplished I might as well have gone back to New York from Kansas City. But I hadn't. First I had dragged out to Excelsior Springs. Then I had charged on to St. Jo. Now, after a glance at a map had shown me, to my intense irritation, that Des Moines was a mere 200 miles or so away, I made a call to the police in that city, introducing myself as John McGrath's campaign manager.

"Oh, yeah, sure I remember," the officer said. "How could I forget? . . . No, she's out now. . . . Funny thing about that. She hung around. Yeah, working as a waitress in a drive-in, for Pete's sake! . . . I don't see why not. Be my guest. It's a free country. Sure thing. Not at all."

The only other person who could conceivably give me any clues as to what was going on was Della DeGraaf, girl whacko and sometime starlet. That variety of scatterbrain could never have dreamed up a sharpshooting act on her own; somebody had to have wound her up and pointed her in the right direction. Maybe I could learn something. Only 200 miles. Only another spoonful. Only a little inchy winchy after that and I could reach the moon. And only charging one little bitty day to vacation time to justify the delay in getting back to Madison Avenue. And for wasting a precious vacation day Jane would only have my teensy brain examined—under a microscope, if necessary, so they could find it.

Della DeGraaf was still pretty, in the way that a high school cheerleader would be pretty if she had been left out in the sun too long and had begun to dissolve. The baby blue eyes were bloodshot and vacant, the china doll complexion had faded and gone slack, and the pert upturned nose bore a nest of blackheads yearning for release. It would be too simple to say only that she had come to be ten years older. The sad fact was that she continued to give off the same empty-headed, gum-chewing, teenage vibes, as if she were still the cutest little thing in town, out there twirling the baton, kicking high, and flashing giant rows of slightly yellowed pearly choppers at the crowd.

In addition, I think her brain had melted, though to be honest I had no idea what it might have been like ten years earlier. She was clearly batty now, but she seemed guileless and almost innocent, and I caught myself liking her for that more than slightly goony charm.

I found her in a short-skirted waitress outfit in a taco palace on the edge of town. When I introduced myself as a "member of the McGrath election team," trying to sound vaguely official but at the same time unthreatening, she looked delighted, no apparent thought that she might ever have done anything wrong crossing her mind. "Oo," she exclaimed, "how is he? I mean them. How is them?" She wrinkled her nose and squealed at her little funny.

"Why don't you have dinner with me after you get off tonight, and I'll tell you all about it?" I suggested. She looked cool and doubtful, suddenly the Hollywood queen fending off unwanted advances. "There's a real good French place in town. Nice enough to be in L.A." That did it. I arranged to pick her up at her room at eight. All I had to do before that was find a real good French place in town.

At dinner she chattered happily about her life and her prospects in Chicago, where the "escort service" she worked for had promised to send her after arrangements had been completed. "They're not so blasé about a movie star in Chicago. You know? I'll really be appreciated there. The boys said they'd be back for me soon."

"Pete and Joe?"

"Yeah. Hey, you know them?"

Yeah, I knew them, and I thought I knew what was happening. It sounded to me like Della DeGraaf's escort service was some sort of reasonably classy call girl outfit, and that she had worn out her usefulness in Los Angeles, a town where almost young, occasionally sober, former nearly movie stars are not entirely in short supply. They had a job for her to do in Des Moines pumping bullets at political candidates and reciting a piece to go along. Maybe they figured just to dump her in Des Moines, there being a reasonable possibility she'd stay put, building a little nest to snuggle down into before she finally realized that nobody was coming to take her nowhere else, not nohow.

But not only was that speculation on my part, it was also a side issue. I got her back to my problem. "Della, I know in your work you got to meet a lot of famous people in L.A., but did you really get a proposal of marriage, the way you said?"

"Yes, I did. Well, sort of, anyway. They said he wanted to marry me—we dated a lot and it was this election business that was stopping it because Mr. and Mrs. Middle America didn't trust real movie stars." She wrinkled her nose in distaste at Des Moines. "So they said, like if I shot a gun in the air, then all that dumb election business would be over and there'd be nothing to stop us from getting married."

I could see someone telling her she'd be doing it for love. "Who's 'they'? Pete and Joey?"

She looked coy. "And some other fellows too. They work for a big company. Coast to coast."

"They give you that gun?"

"Uh huh." She looked anxious. "But they told me to shoot up in the air and not try to hurt anybody. And hey, I shouldn't even be talking about this. They told me not to."

"I won't tell a soul, Della, and there's not much more I want to ask you anyway." At least something was clear. That gun had been stolen in Boston and supplied by Pierre LeGrand's people; Della was right in saying she was tied in with a coast-to-coast company. "Let me get this straight. The people you work for said that if you did this little job then you'd be able to get married after it all blew over?"

She nodded. "That's right. And meantime, I could work for the organization in Chicago, and in case I didn't get married, I could stay there. It'd be much more fun than Los Angeles."

I supposed it wasn't inconceivable that John McGrath had availed himself of Della's services at some time or other when he had been in Los Angeles, but more than that I couldn't imagine. "Tell me, Della, this must have been a real whirlwind romance, hey?"

"It was." She smiled modestly.

"Why don't you give me the lowdown? Your friends wouldn't mind that. How many times did you and John McGrath really date before he proposed to you? Sort of proposed."

She lay down her knife and fork and looked horrified. I wondered if the kitchen had incompletely thawed the fresh, cooked-to-order, frozen Noisettes de Veau, Périgourdine. "John? Not John! He's an old man! *George* McGrath. *George* and I were going to get married! Gee, mister, how dumb can you get? George and I used to go out lots together!" She bridled, as if I had accused her of an indecency, of leading on a poor old gentleman like George's father.

"George?" I repeated weakly, "you and George?"

"Well, half a dozen times, anyway. But when it's the right guy and the chemistry is there, that's all it takes. He wanted to propose, I could tell, but he was afraid of his father and so he didn't. You see, Mr. and Mrs. Middle America—"

"You already told me. I understand. If George didn't have to be the president's son, you and he could get married. Is that right?"

She nodded, pleased that at last I understood. "Soon as this election stuff was over."

"So, if you helped things along a little with that gun they gave you, then if anything went wrong with you and George, at least you'd have that job in Chicago."

"Now you've got it."

"Thank you, Della. Tell me, how did you and George meet?"

"It was at a big party. He was all by himself and he looked lonely, so the fellow who brought me said I ought to go cheer him up."

"At a big party. That must have been swell."

"Oh, it sure was. This fancy place right in Marina de la Reina. At George's sister's house."

"You mean you know Eileen McGrath too?"

"No, not exactly. I mean, I was sort of introduced to her, but there was lots of people there. I bet she didn't know half the guests. You know how it is in the movie world. Very informal. It's like family, people just sort of bring their friends along. Even their own cocaine in case there isn't any." She preened herself, in love with her own glamorous self. "You understand."

I didn't understand, but I said I did anyway. The interconnections and twists and turns were making me feel as if I were living through something endless, like at least six out of the seven books of Marcel Proust. I was going to end up as addled as my dinner companion, if this kept up.

Fortunately, however, that was all I learned that evening, which saved me from succumbing to brain fever.

I knew that now I had everything I needed to solve the puzzle, but I still wasn't able to put the pieces together. What Hank Beeler and Anna McGrath and Della DeGraaf had told me added up to a solution, if only I had been able to add. One side issue was indisputably clear, though. Della had been set up to put the make on George. I was sure the boy hadn't actually proposed to her, just as I was sure that somebody had convinced Della that he wanted to propose and that he really and truly would, if she would just take care of a few small obstacles by firing a gun. Della, without being clear in her own little head about it, had vaguely sensed that marriage to George was a way out of a blind alley, no matter how successful she was in deluding herself that she was about to be proclaimed queen of all the Chicagos. So she had jumped at the chance.

I took her back to her rooming house after dinner, and as I watched her trip happily up the steps and turn to wave goodbye to us adoring throngs below, I became sure of something else: Della DeGraaf had been dumped. Nobody was going to set her up in Chicago, and they weren't going to ferry her back to Los Angeles either. Yet I had the idea that in an environment without the glitter dust to confuse her, she might find a reasonable way of life. Marry a trucker or something. She just might. And then again, she might not. But I liked the notion of Della and some guy turning into Mr. and Mrs. Middle America and looking down their noses at Hollywood.

TWENTY-TWO

There was a connection for New York out of Des Moines late that night and I took it despite the gnawing fear that leaving Des Moines late at night might get to be a habit. By the time I reached New York I knew I wasn't going to go to the taxi stand and point myself toward Manhattan. Instead, I phoned Al Delaney in Manchester. "Hiya, kid," he said, "long time no see." He laughed maniacally; the campaign was clearly getting to the man.

"Cut the comedy, Al. Listen, I've got to see George McGrath. I know he left town. Where is he? This is important."

"I didn't know he left, because he's sure as hell back here now, whimpering to be let in the back door to help his daddy. Some help. And why in the name of sanity would you want to see that piece of bad news?"

"Never mind that. Just keep him there, will you? Put him on a leash if you have to. And, say, do me a big personal favor and give Ed Jorgensen a call. Tell him you got hold of me in Kansas City because you wanted me back in Manchester. And tell him you called me yesterday, okay?" There was no point in not retrieving that day I had so extravagantly squandered as vacation time, not when my error in judgment could so easily be corrected. As Anna McGrath might have put it, a little white lie never hurt anybody. "I'll explain when I see you."

"Yeah, sure. I'll take care of it. One thing, though. Johnny's been making speeches about how he fired his pollster because he wants the voters to see the real John McGrath or some such horseshit. Like you suggested, though if you ask me I still think it stinks. So if you're fired like Johnny says, wear a heavy veil when you get off the plane up here, right? We wouldn't want to make a liar out of our man, would we."

"Heck, no. Not when they can do it so much better by themselves, all those pols. But okay, you keep hold of George, I'll wear more veils than an ayatollah's two best girlfriends." I hung up and scuttled through the curvy byways of LaGuardia looking for something that flew to Manchester.

When I finally reached New Hampshire I found that my favorite motel had cunningly contrived to save the same home away from home for me, view of the kitchen slops buckets and all. I dumped my bag on the run and loped over to campaign headquarters. Luck was with me; sitting there in all his pasty-faced glory was boy George gluing clippings into a book—they had found something harmless and useful for him to do, and it kept him indoors and out of trouble.

"Whatever you're doing, George, drop it. I want to talk to you." I raised a hand to cut off his protest. "Shut up and come with me. This is more important. Come on, boy, let's move!" He rose from his seat and complied meekly, a docile spaniel trotting in my wake. I guessed that he'd been conditioned by the iron lady of St. Jo so that on command he'd sit up, shake hands, roll over, or play dead.

I led him into an emptyish coffee shop and jutted my chin toward a booth in the rear. "Now," I said, after I had ordered coffee and danish for two without consulting my guest, and in the full knowledge that he would have preferred a beverage with a higher octane rating, "listen to me. I'm almost certainly the only fool on God's green earth who thinks that you're actually trying to help your father, even though you've managed to screw things up royally every chance you've had. Shut up." His lips flopped together as mushily as those of a hand puppet as I cut off his protest. "I'm going to ask a couple of questions, and I want straight answers. You give 'em to me without crapping around and you'll be helping your dad and you'll be helping yourself. You understand?" He didn't understand, but he nodded uncertainly anyway.

"Good. First, when did you leave Manchester and why? Come on, talk. I know you were out of town."

"The morning after that fire, real early. I don't know what time but it was early morning. I wasn't helping Dad here so I thought the best thing I could do was just leave. All I did here was make trouble."

If he wanted me to contradict that last remark he was going to have to wait a long time. But since I had seen him leave that morning, when he was arguing with the hood, I knew I was getting the truth, at least to begin with. "Where'd you go?"

"Albany."

"*Albany!* For God's sake, why Albany?"

"I didn't want anybody to know where I was so nobody could make trouble, sort of, and Albany's pretty close to here. I mean, if nobody could find me, nobody could trip me up."

"You mean like they did in the bar, when you got tossed out for the TV cameras?"

"Yeah. I said I was going to Boston, but I went to Albany. Albany stinks, if you wanna know."

"Okay, so you went into hiding. What brought you back, and when?"

"Yesterday. The campaign's about over here, and anyway, they said Dad was going to lose. I just wanted to be with him, that's all." He hung his head and blushed.

I believed him; the blush was prime Lillian Gish, and totally convincing. And I was reasonably sure I had proof that George McGrath couldn't have told anybody that I had a copy of the computer runs with me when I left for Woodstock. I was also beginning to get some idea about how Barbara Jellthrop came to be wandering around the woods without shoes. But there was more I needed from this hapless child before I moved on.

"That's the easy part, George. Now it gets tougher." His chin, or at any rate a selection of his chins, quivered as he swallowed. "When you were looking at the clippings about the woman who took a potshot at your father in Des Moines, how come you jumped up and ran out like that?"

"I don't know. No special reason. It was like, well, I got so upset, that's all. I mean, what the hell!"

I shook my head. "Oh, George, George, that's bullshit, and we both know it. I'm disappointed in you. Let me put it to you another way: How long have you known Della DeGraaf?"

"Oh," he said, "you know."

"That's right: 'Oh, I know.' So stop crapping around. I'm on your side, kid, so let's have it straight."

He hung his head. "Maybe seven, eight months."

"Met her at Eileen's, didn't you?" I might as well give him the idea there was lots I knew, so he wouldn't go all coy on me again.

He looked startled. "How'd you know that?"

"I just know. Date her a lot, did you?"

"I guess. She kept calling me, and, heck, she was fun, so I guess I saw a lot of her. Sort of, anyway."

"I'll bet." Poor slob. No girl had ever pursued him, and he never expected one would. And this one was a movie star—sort of, nearly, practically. "And you proposed to her, huh?"

"Oh, no! No way did I propose. I don't care what anybody says, I never did. She practically proposed to me, for God's sake! She kept hinting, talking about how she was ready to settle down, but I never went along with it, so help me. No way did I propose," he repeated strongly.

How could I disbelieve what had to be one of the firmest, most categorical statements George had ever uttered in his life? I believed. Somebody else had planted the idea in that girl's unfocused birdbrain that the boy wanted to marry her, if only the chance of his father getting elected president wasn't about to interfere. I wondered briefly if Della had ever made a movie about the unrequited love of a prince for a milkmaid, or, given the lady, a prince and a fermented milkmaid.

"Are you dead certain about that?" I asked. "You never gave her even the slightest hint that you'd marry her if things were different? I mean just to quiet her down? This is the most important question I have to get an answer to if you and I are going to help your father, if we're going to stop this smear campaign, not just here in New Hampshire, but in the rest of the country as well. So think hard before you answer."

"So help me," George said. "She kept saying we were a great team, how we ought to stick together. But you know, she was always half pissed. Even worse than me," he mumbled, looking down at the table top. "I couldn't, even if I wanted to. I mean, after what drink did to Ma—and heck, she was even older than me. I'd just never—" He broke off. "And my grandma—" I knew what he meant. If he had ever brought Della DeGraaf into that St. Jo bungalow, Granny would have put him across her knees, unbuttoned the seat of his union suit, and whaled the tar out of him.

"Okay, now, take it easy. Pull yourself together, and let's keep going." I gave him a moment to take a couple of deep breaths, and when he surfaced again I recommenced. "The next thing is those two cruddy types I kept seeing you with, Pete and Joe. The day you left you gave one of them an envelope out in front of the motel." He looked startled. "It had money in it, didn't it?" He nodded. "Okay, suppose you tell me what that was all about. What were you paying those two for? You put them up to something, didn't you? Let's have it, and keep it simple; no apologies, no explanations. Just say it."

"Put them up to something! You're crazy! Listen, I wasn't paying them, I was paying them off! They were going to drag Della into this again. They were going to put it out that she was *my* girl, not Dad's, and that was something that could stick and that they could prove. Hell, half the bartenders in L.A. shoveled me and Della out the door dead drunk, one time or another. They said they'd really fix Dad, that people'd love a story about me and Dad going after the same girl. And they could do it!"

"Did you really believe that?" I asked, not hiding the scorn in my voice. "Do you think those two bums could do that?"

"Yeah," he said, for once standing up to me, "I really believe that. Who do you think got me tossed out of that bar? Who do you think got the TV cameras there, waiting for me in the street, Dan Rather? Yeah, I believe those two bums could do that."

Well, I thought, I'll be damned! The kid was standing up to me. Maybe there was hope for him yet. For the first time since I had laid eyes on him, I felt a small twitch of respect for the poor dummy, though I did my best to keep it down. But he was really doing something for his old man, and he was keeping shut up about it until I forced it into the open, letting the rest of us jump up and down on his mattressy carcass without complaint. It was time to go a little easier on him, especially since everything was falling into place for me. "Just a couple more things, George, and no more rough ones," I said. "I'm puzzled about you and Eileen. I thought she couldn't stand the sight of you, but she had you to this party back in California."

Having quieted me with his first explosion, he felt encouraged to do it again. "*You're* puzzled! Hell, what do you think *I* am? I don't know what's going on with that one. I used to visit her maybe half a dozen times a year, stay with her, even. Sure, we'd have fights, she thought I was a washout and I thought she was too damn feisty, but we didn't get along all that bad. That's what I thought, but how wrong can a guy get? I show up in Manchester, she's ready to kill me. Damn her, anyway. I can't help you figure what's up with that one. She's just nuts."

"That's okay. You've helped. You may not know it but you've helped a hell of a lot. And after I take care of something, I don't think you're going to be in any more trouble with your two buddies in Manchester or anywhere else during this campaign unless you really work at bringing it on yourself. Go on back to headquarters now, and I'll be seeing you around. Don't you worry about a thing, I promise you. Just you go back; I'm sticking here a while longer."

He got up to go. "Oh, hey," I said, "there's one thing I forgot to ask you. You know that survey that got burned up in the fire?" He nodded. "Okay. When did you first find out that I had run off a set of tabulations before the fire ruined everything, and that I had taken them down to Woodstock with me?"

He looked at me, that damn fool lip hanging down again. "I don't know what you're talking about. What tabulations? And what's Woodstock got to do with it? You mean where they had that rock festival?"

"Yep, that's the place, all right, and that's the answer I

figured you'd give me. Forget it, George. Everything's great. You've told me what I need to know."

The boy left. I watched that chubby, unattractive profile waddle past the coffee shop window, and I felt sad. God knows why. But I had more important things to brood about. Now I was pretty sure I knew a lot, such as what was fueling this campaign against Johnny, though I was far from absolute certainty. I had to think about what to do next.

So I thought, which is usually, if not always, a bad idea. Then I went back to the motel, got a piece of stationery, and sat down at the desk in my room. "Dear Mr. LeGrand," I started, "I have the idea that if I came down to Boston to see you, I might never be allowed upstairs into your office, so I'm taking the opportunity to write about a few things I'm sure will interest you. . . ." After I penned a couple of paragraphs, I wound up with, "If you'd be at all interested in hearing more, please call me at the motel number on the letterhead and I'll be right down. Or, if you would prefer to send your car for me, I'd not be averse to riding in it again." I signed my name and took the letter to the post office, where I sent it certified to addressee only. By overnight mail.

One of four things had to happen next. Mr. LeGrand could ignore me, figuring I could drop dead for all he cared. Two, I would be setting out for Boston in a rental car. Three, I would be riding off in a long black car with a built-in bar. Or four, I might be transported in a different kind of long black car, one with lots of flowers, followed by Jane wearing matching black—in case LeGrand decided I wasn't dropping dead fast enough. I had one other thought: Could I get the letter back from the post office? No, I answered myself; better and simpler to try stopping potential bullets with my bare hands than to try retrieving a missive already stamped, certified, and sent.

TWENTY-THREE

I could hear the sound of a typewriter being whacked when I knocked on Eileen's door. "Hi," I said, ever so casually, "Al told me I'd find you here. What're you up to? Can I come in?"

She glanced hurriedly at her watch. "Sure. It's just that I've got to get this article off this afternoon. But come on in for a bit. What's up? I thought you'd left us."

"I did, but there are a couple of things to tidy up, so I'm back. Not much, though, and then I'll be off again."

"Me too. Only a day and a half before the vote. There's not much any of us can do now, and I've got to get on with this thing. I promised an article on the role of women in the primaries."

"Well, you've done a lot. You should know."

"I hope so."

Then I said, "And if you write about it in that article, it ought to do a lot for the feminist cause. Like set it back about fifty years."

She sat up straight, surprised, not knowing how to take that. "That's not very funny, Ev."

"It wasn't meant to be very funny."

"Come on, cut it out. I've got work to do."

"Come on yourself. You've done your work, ma'am. Too damned well, that's how you've done it. You've lost your father the election, so you can relax now. Tell me," I asked, taking a cue from that drunken night with Betty Gold, "do you hate all the boys or only the ones in the family? Or does the truth lie somewhere in between, as it so often does? You'll have to excuse it if I sound like a ten-cent Freud, but that's all this case is worth."

She flicked off the typewriter and turned to face me directly. "Get your ass out of here, will you? I've got no time for games. Explain yourself or get out. No. I'll take that back. Explain yourself *and* get out."

"Okay," I said mildly, "that's a reasonable request." I looked at the picture over the bed as I composed my thoughts; it was something disgusting involving sheep, a collie, and a shepherdess sweet enough to make your teeth ache. I tried to imagine that the little doll was headed for a sex party with a gang of shepherds somewhere down the lane and that the sheep were supposed to stand guard, but I couldn't bring the idea, pleasant though it was, into focus. "Somebody knew a lot about the dirty linen in your father's closet, or thought they did, somebody as close as you or George. But George got it all wrong; he didn't think there was any dirt. He thought your father had nothing to do with your mother's drinking, and living with your grandmother he didn't have any notion that there were any other women along the way. Your grandmother saved him from that knowledge."

"George usually gets things wrong. So what?"

"So I think you decided that this man had gotten away with enough. He destroyed your mother, according to you, and he walked away from the remains. Now he was about to try to make himself king of the hill. Like all men. In fact, I think you got him mixed up with all men, Eileen. Anyway, be that as it may, he wasn't going to get off scot free, not that easy, not while you were around to see to it."

She looked at me, her head slightly to one side, her lips parted and an expression of scorn on her face. Her nails were still curled over the typewriter keys like a vulture's talons over a mouse. "That's interesting. Now you've explained. Thank you, and goodbye. Get out." She flipped the typewriter on. "Go on, fuck off, Franklin."

"Only you made one mistake. Your mother was on the sauce long before she met your father, she was on it when they were married, she's still on it, and he had very little to do with it."

"That's a crock. And don't you talk that way about her, either."

"I've met her. I know what's a crock and what isn't. And by the way, I mean no disrespect. She's a damn sight nicer than her kids. And oh, yes, she sends her regards. I think she'd even like to see you, for God's sake. With all that righteous fury on her account, I still would bet you haven't been out to Excelsior Springs in over a year. Right?"

By way of answer she picked up the dictionary next to the typewriter and chucked it at me. "Thanks," I said, "but I already know the words: hypocritical, vindictive, sneaky. And, oh, yeah, wrong." I picked the book up and tossed it back. She made no move to deflect it as it hit her leg and fell to the floor. "And then you tried to pin it on George. Poor, dumb, unattractive George, the family patsy. Even without help from you, not worth much. A natural fall guy for the asking.

"For a while I was fooled about the boy. I thought he was behind what was going on, hanging out with those seamy types, getting tossed out of bars with the cameras ready in advance, and generally acting as if he was trying to stir up trouble. Hell, I even saw him give money to one of those crooks and I thought he was paying them to make waves. Now I know he wasn't; he was paying them off, which is a horse's ass of a different color, no? Blackmail. He was the one tied in with the DeGraaf girl, not your father, and you knew it. What a pretty story it would have made if George hadn't bought them off—the kid and the old man both chasing the same piece of expensive tail. It could have been sensational. Who would have thought that George would ever rear himself high enough on his hind legs to pay off these guys, not just sit there cringing and let it happen. You want to know how I figured it was you, not George?"

"No. You're delirious, you son of a bitch, and I don't know what you're talking about. What's more, neither do you. But from that shit-eating grin on your face, I think you're going to tell me anyway."

"Damn right. Because you knew I was taking that last survey data down to Woodstock with me, and George didn't. He left town before Al Delaney got my note that I had a copy of the computer runs, the only copy run off before the fire, and that I was going off with them. Al told everybody in town, but he couldn't have told George because George was in Albany. Albany, for God's sake! So it was you who told your little chums that if they wanted to be sure Daddy didn't get off the ground again they might think about relieving me of the stuff, for whatever it was worth.

"What I don't understand," I admitted, "is how you arranged it all. How'd you get it set up? That's a mighty big organization you've got working for you. Pierre LeGrand, no less. How does an ordinary Josephine even get in touch? Up to there I think I understand. But that's when I get lost."

"Really. Well, get lost some more. Permanently. Get out of here!" She stood, her arms rigid at her sides and her fists clenched. Her face was flushed, and the red glow extended down across her neck as if she were standing over an open fire. With a quantum leap in time she became her own dear granny, righteous indignation flooding into a twisted, bitter mouth. She panted, panted as if she had been running uphill for years without pause, which in a sense I figured she had.

"Okay," I said, "calm down. I'm off. I kind of thought you might not believe me, so I wrote down your grandfather's phone number. I mean, I was pretty sure you didn't dial it often enough to know it by heart. Go ahead, why don't you call him? Ask about your mother—he'll tell you—and have a little chat. Maybe find out about the weather in Missouri; that's always safe. I'll be back in half an hour. If you want to let me in, that's fine. If you don't, that's okay too. Either way, I won't insist, I promise you. You can count on that.

"And another thing you can count on is that there's going to be a price to pay, lady. You've dumped on your father and your brother both, and there's toxic waste enough to cover New Jersey twice. Now you're going to have to do something about dumping without a permit, dolly; nothing's for free." I held out the paper I had written Hank Beeler's phone number on. Eileen raised her arms, fists still clenched, and clutched them both to her chest, stiff as an Egyptian statue. "Have it your way," I said, and I flicked the paper toward her. She made no move to grab it.

As I walked out I caught a glimpse of her looking down. One fist was open, and her hand was extended over the paper. She could have been pronouncing a benediction or muttering a malediction. I'd be the last to know which.

I returned to my own room to lie down until it was curtain time for Act Two. I was winded, my heart was pounding, and my stomach was making noises like an over-age West Side subway car making a sharp turn faster than the safety limit. I rooted about in my suitcase for the antacid tablets that make a home there and popped one. My eyes closed and I thought that if Eileen didn't crack, if she called my bluff and didn't tell me how she managed to mount the campaign to destroy her father, I'd never know. But two things were for sure. I was going to stop her, even though it might be too late to save Johnny by now. And I knew how and why and because of whom Barbara Jellthrop had met her death. I'd never be able to prove it, but I thought I could do someone a dirty turn by cueing Pierre LeGrand into the sideline his minions Pete and Joe had been exploiting. I know the Lord claimed vengeance for himself, but I never knew him to object to a little help from his friends. After all, Mohammed was an expert at moving mountains, but if someone had shown up with a bulldozer he might have been touched by the gesture.

Half an hour later I knocked on Eileen's door again. I rapped twice and said, "It's me. You want to let me in?" Thirty seconds went by on my watch, and forty-six thumps in my heart. Nothing stirred. I had visions of the girl standing straight, fists still clenched, knuckle-white, motionless, sculpted ice, even the burning hatred turned frigid. As I turned to leave, the door opened. She nodded almost imperceptibly, her face the color of a skating pond on a cloudy day.

"I called my grandfather," she told me in a voice that came out of a dream, detached and distant.

"And?"

"You know already. My mother. It's not his fault, not my father's fault, Grandpa says. He says that years before, Mother—" She looked at me sharply, life and fury both returning to her eyes. "I still say that he made it worse. If he hadn't started catting around—"

"Do tell," I said. "Which is he, the chicken or the egg?

If he hadn't started catting around she wouldn't have started drinking and if she hadn't started drinking he wouldn't have started—hell, you get the idea, don't you?"

She answered with another question. "What do you want from me, Ev? Why are you doing this?" Her eyes were either defiant or pleading. "What's it to you?"

"I don't know. Not yet. I honestly don't. But before anything else, I want some straight answers." She nodded. "How did you get this organized, to begin with. Most people, for God's sake, they wouldn't know how to find a butcher guaranteed to give short weight, much less latch onto a whole outfit that makes big business out of crime. How'd you get hold of Pierre LeGrand, a classified ad in the L.A. *Times*?"

Her face twisted impatiently. "That was incidental. It just happened. You know I've got this guy living with me?" I nodded. "Well, when Dad got into the race, I said he didn't deserve to win, that I'd love to be able to screw it up for him. It was only talk. At least at first it was only talk. I didn't mean anything by it, but Andy, that's his name, he had connections, he'd get the stuff we wanted sometimes, like, you know, cocaine—"

"You mean like cocaine, or you mean cocaine?" I asked, not much sympathy in my voice.

She looked at me coldly. "You know damn well what I mean, and I can do without that. Anyway, there's a lot of money bet on these campaigns, and somebody figured they could rake in a bundle if a leading candidate suddenly lost out in a big way. They came to me with this proposition. Through Andy. I'd give them as much dirt as I could on Dad, the kind that could be proved, things with names, dates, and witnesses. And they wanted me to set it up so George would meet this DeGraaf freak. Then they said they could take it from there."

"Easy as that, huh?"

She laughed, a sort of a bark coming out of her mouth,

but I knew it was a laugh because her mouth was open and her teeth were showing. "Uh huh, that's what I thought. That's what they wanted me to think. They knew New Hampshire was crucial, and I told them Dad wasn't planning to get the nomination but to come in second. That was all they needed to know. They handled it out of their Boston subsidiary"—here, the same bark issued forth and the teeth showed again between her drawn-back lips—"as if they were General Motors. New Hampshire, it seems, was in the Boston territory. And listen," she said urgently, "I didn't know they were going to have that woman shoot at Dad. I swear I didn't. You believe me, don't you?"

She stepped over and put those icy claws on my arms, and I could feel her nails dig in through my jacket. Before I realized it, or, to be charitable, before either of us realized it, her arms were around my neck and we were pressed hard against each other. Her hips ground in, ever so slightly, not enough for an X rating. An upper thigh pushed insistently between my legs, and as I felt that wonderful knee-weakening warmth spreading up and down from the pit of my stomach, I ground back. Slowly, gently, the two of us swayed, nothing an eyewitness could have sworn to in court with any certainty. My hands slid down her back and I could feel those luscious hams harden and flex.

Then, damn it, her hips rolled with a greater urgency and I thought of Betty Gold's lecture on Miss McGrath and her tennis shorts, and the spell was smashed. I backed off. "You were saying, Eileen?" In recollection, I believe my voice was hoarse.

Our grand passion deflated, she picked up even more calmly than when she had broken off, as if the momentary lapse was to be politely ignored, like someone farting in an elevator. "They goofed. Like every damned big bureaucracy, they got it wrong. The West Coast told them in Boston that the girl had a hold on McGrath, that he'd been banging her, that there was any number of witnesses. The

West meant George, of course, the East thought they were talking about John and sent those two goons from Boston to pick her up and ferry her to Des Moines. Cattle trucked to the Eastern market. I don't know what kind of story they gave her, but she's so dotty they could have convinced her that if she took a shot at the Dalai Lama she could marry the Pope.

"That's when I began to get scared. It had gotten away from me. No, that's wrong: They had taken it away from me. They didn't need me anymore. When I saw how they were using George to destroy my father, and how the poor sap kept sticking his head in the noose, begging to be strung up, almost, the way they got him drunk, got him thrown out of bars into the arms of the press, I felt so sorry for him that I hated him. What an easy, stupid mark, the poor slob!"

So Eileen had came to hate her brother because of the rage she felt toward herself and had to turn outward on someone else, someone she was using as an instrument of her hate.

"I knew it was wrong by then, but I was in over my head, and I couldn't stop the damn thing. Look," she said sharply, "I'm not apologizing or trying to excuse anything. I still wanted to keep him from getting that nomination. But not that way, not anymore. It's been a nightmare, and it's still not over. It goes on, unless he gets his second place in New Hampshire and those people decide to cut their losses."

"Don't get your hopes up, Eileen. He's not going to get that second place, and if there's anything after last place, that's where he'll wind up."

"I know. What can I do?"

"Nothing, I hope. Squirm. After you've shot the man down, don't come to me for absolution. Try your spiritual adviser. Maybe he'll suggest a bath with strong soap, or maybe he'll throw up." I turned to leave.

"You going to tell him, tell my father?"

"I don't know yet. I don't know what I'm going to do."

She stretched a hand toward me. It may have been the closest she had ever come to pleading for something. I refrained from spitting in it, but for the moment that was all the charity I could muster. I closed the door behind me before I could change my mind. Then I headed for the bar; alcohol is a marvelous antiseptic when you're feeling soiled.

TWENTY-FOUR

There was time to kill. Another day, and if I hadn't heard from Pierre LeGrand I wasn't going to hear from Pierre LeGrand. That would be the end of my involvement in the Barbara Jellthrop case because the police weren't going to listen to my madness, and I had no intention of making a fool of myself for their jollification by spinning a web of dotty suppositions.

For the moment, waiting for LeGrand, I loafed. Since somebody ought to have been working hard to serve the interests of Finch, Rowan, & Hyde, I decided to see how Betty and Bill were coming along. I took a note to the reception desk to leave for Betty. The clerk looked at it and then informed me, "Miss Gold says if anybody's looking for her she's in the rec room on the lower level."

And so she was. Loafing, just like me. Bill was there,

and he was loafing too. In fact, I interrupted their game of Ping-Pong, which a couple of ten-year-olds who wanted the equipment themselves were watching unhappily. "Good thing Ed Jorgensen isn't here to see you two," I said.

"Why?" Betty asked. "Doesn't old Ed like Ping-Pong? I'm sorry, but the room's too small for a softball game." She put her paddle down. "Anyway, I'm glad to see you. Any excuse to stop. This guy's beating the hell out of me."

"One more volley," Toscani begged, and he proceeded to serve. He slammed the ball like a killer. Betty managed to return it twice, but she never had a chance. When it was over, the victor crowed, "Okay, that's point, game, set, tournament, ten bucks, and that thing you promised in Macy's window." I realized that even an account man, driven mad by a lifetime of polishing clients' toenails, and a second eternity of taking them to fancy restaurants to watch them flood the *gigot farci en croûte* with chili sauce, needed to lash out at someone once in a while. My respect for him doubled, which is saying something, though not very much.

"Don't rub it in," Betty said. "I ache all over, which covers a lot of ground." To me, she added, "We've been playing since yesterday morning, and that's more exercise than I've had since three days after I got married."

"Lovely," I said, "but don't I remember something about a campaign you're working on? A political campaign? Like for some guy named McGrath?"

"You'd think so, wouldn't you? But we're sort of semi-sacked, like you except without the humiliation of all those public announcements. He's doing it his way. Bill and I were on a conference call to the office with McGrath and with half the copywriters back in town. He threw out most of the stuff we had for him. Got his new act underway, and he's not paying much attention to the agency."

"You've got to admit it isn't bad," Bill said. "'I'll do it my way.' That's his theme these days."

"Yeah," Betty added. "It ought to be 'The Wrath of McGrath,' for God's sake! He practically says whatever he damn pleases. Yesterday he told a church supper that Duckworth can't remember whether he's working for God or God is working for him. And he's talking like political pollsters are the Great Satan." She grinned at me evilly. "I will say, though, the son of a bitch may be going out, but he's going out in style."

"How's he doing? How's he going over?" I asked.

They both spoke together. "Who can tell?" "Gets wild applause, but there's always lots of people love to hear things like that."

"Well, if McGrath isn't using you, what've you two been doing?"

Toscani snorted and looked at Betty almost prissily, which is a very rare way indeed for a Madison Avenue pitchman to look. "Oh, come on," Betty objected, "it's not all that bad." She turned to me. "I met a couple of the locals, that's all, and this guy here thinks there's something wrong with that. I mean, with nothing else to do, what do you expect? I couldn't sit in the room all day watching television, could I? Hey, you know, Ev, the boys around here are pretty damn much up to date, more than I would have guessed."

Toscani, adrip with disapproval, observed, "What she means is that some type in the bar asked her to join him in his hot tub. Party, party."

"Well, I turned him down, didn't I? What do you want from me?" She turned to me. "You see what I mean about getting a reputation for nothing?"

"You must have said something. What was it?" I asked weakly.

"Oh, nothing much. Honestly! Just that I never get into hot tubs with strange men unless they've bought the optional built-in automatic dingleberry strainer attachment.

So the guy left. Big deal. What do you want from me?" She glowered at Toscani.

I said, "I'm not sure I'm old enough for much more of this. What now? You still have to hang around?"

"Nope," Bill said. "We're off. Bags packed. Party's over, thank God. There's a plane at six."

"You want to come with us?" Betty asked.

"I guess not. There're still a couple of loose ends for me to hang myself with. See you in the office."

I wandered over to Havemeyer's headquarters. He had the lion's share of the party's money behind him, and consequently had the classiest polling setup of any of the candidates. Lehman-Thornton were his pollsters, and they ranked up there with Roper, Harris, and Gallup. Everybody in polling knows everybody else, and I found my counterpart, Pauline Freund, looking not too busy. I pried her loose for some information.

"How's it going, Polly?"

"Same. My guy's way out front. It's so easy, I'm bored. This point, he could read a laundry list to them and turn up a three percent gain in the polls. Say, Ev, I hear you've been sacked. True, untrue, or don't know?"

"You know damn well it's true, what with McGrath hooting it from a platform whenever he can get a crowd of three people together. You trying to be funny?"

She grinned evilly, but then all the girls were grinning evilly today. "No, but there's something that isn't very funny that's making all us polling types look foolish. McGrath has been saying for, what, three, four days? that from now on he's speaking for himself, no pollster's dummy, he. Right? Well, damn it to hell, it's working! He's creeping up again! I don't mean he's ahead, but he's moved enough to show up in the polls. Ev, dear, I don't think you and I and our kind are very popular with the general public."

"No kidding. Is Havemeyer going to talk about it?"

"I doubt it. Why should he? It'd only encourage the knee-jerk sympathy for the underdog vote to go all out for your boy again, and Havemeyer's not about to give the opposition a hand. Funny thing, isn't it, the way people don't trust us. And you know, it's working like out of a text book: The farm vote, where the morals are dug in solid, they still think your guy's a turd, but the urban paranoiacs who are always looking over their shoulders to see who's creeping up on them, they're the ones who figure somebody's trying to con them, and they're loving this bull about McGrath dumping his pollsters. This business about standing up and shouting no to the guys who are trying to manipulate people—it's working, Ev. It's a lot of nonsense, but it's working."

"Well, I'll be damned."

"Probably. But don't get your hopes up. He's still way down there."

"You think he's got a chance? I mean, just for second place, maybe."

"Yes," she said. "Or no. Or don't know. I'd be the last to know." She pursed her lips and thought. "Next to last. *You'd* be the last to know. Look, honey, it's been grand knowing you, but I've got to get back to work. Havemeyer's coming in any minute now so's I can tell him whether to scratch his left nut or the right one when he talks to the Conservative Club. I gotta get ready. I wouldn't want to be fired by anything as low as a politician. Like some people I could name."

I wondered if Pierre LeGrand knew that the McGrath candidacy might still be alive. Probably not, since that was one aspect of the polls no other candidate would talk about. And Johnny, without his own polls anymore, wouldn't have the facts in hand either, which gave me cause for a certain negative satisfaction.

Instead of thinking about what I could do, and why I shouldn't do it, I went to a movie, something with pirates.

The main difference between them and politicians is that it's the rare politician who wears a patch over his eye, while your everyday buccaneer doesn't generally smoke cigars.

After the show I scurried back through the bone-chilling cold to the motel. One more night in Manchester, and if there was still no word from LeGrand, I'd drop it and go home to the relatively tropical shores of New York. At least down there I got paid for minding somebody else's business. But outside the motel I saw a long, black limo that told me I was about to go off to Boston. If I hadn't seen that apartment-sized vehicle I never would have spotted my buddy Pete in the lobby, since he had vastly upgraded his decor by going to sleep with a newspaper over his face.

I touched him on the shoulder, through the paper, to keep my fingers clean. "You looking for me?" I asked.

He took off the paper and folded the page with great deliberation before answering. It was the obituary column; maybe he hadn't finished it yet. "Yeah. Too damn late now. Pick you up eight inna morning. You be ready." He got up and left, infuriatingly confident that I wasn't going to lay claim to a prior engagement.

I stared after his manly back, wishing I could think of a retort. "Yah, so's yer old man!" was all I could come up with, so I went to bed instead.

TWENTY-FIVE

LeGrand received me more formally this time, meaning he was dressed. He wore a dark gray pinstripe suit with the jacket a tad shorter than American style, the way Italian tailors do it; shoes that looked soft enough to have occupied an Eskimo family for months of chewing the leather into submission; a multiwidth striped shirt that was probably too expensive for Turnbull and Asser to market; and a tie whose muted intricacies would have turned Sulka dizzy with impotent envy. "So good to see you again, Mr. Franklin," he said with a smile. "Please sit. Cigar? Or is it too early for you? Coffee?"

"Just coffee, I think." I wanted that cigar badly, if only as a souvenir, but I felt strangely that taking one would have signified the loss of a skirmish. And I didn't even know if there was a skirmish for me to lose. I've been that way ever since I was an office boy at a company Christmas party a thousand years ago. The boss, who owned the joint, sat next to the expensive hors d'oeuvres platter of shrimp and oysters and beamed with pseudofatherly approval at all who helped themselves, so for reasons I couldn't have expressed at the time I stayed with the celery sticks stuffed with processed American cheese, thus consummating the only victory I have had over management in a long career in the business world.

LeGrand flipped on the intercom and got the coffee detail into action. Then we chatted. And chatted. He asked about Jane and Billy, about whom he possessed an alarming amount of knowledge. He told me about his wife and the son who would take over when the retirement plans were activated in the very near future. It was like a transaction with a Japanese corporate executive, no sordid details to come up before the amenities were concluded. At long last, after the necessary courtesies and I had both been thoroughly exhausted, my host observed, "Your letter, it was very interesting. Intriguing, even."

"Thank you. I hoped it would get your attention."

"Oh, it did, Mr. Franklin, it did. Though speaking only for myself, I would never have put anything like that on paper. The wrong hands, and"—he shrugged expressively—"and *Zap!* as they say in the comic strips. You understand."

"I understand. But I didn't think you'd be letting it get into the wrong hands, Mr. LeGrand."

"Ah? And if I myself am the wrong hands?" He smiled, benevolent as a crocodile at feeding time. "Rest assured, I'm not. I want only to impress you with the need for discretion regarding anything you may say or hear me say in this room. To be frank, at this point you want something from me. I need nothing from you, though I admit to some curiosity. We understand each other?"

I nodded. "We understand each other."

"Good!" He rubbed his hands together, signifying, perhaps, the beginning of the feast. "Now, to start with the most unfortunate item, the death of the young girl. As you realized, while my men were destroying your survey room, your computers, those tapes—I comprehend these things only dimly—the young Jellthrop girl walked in. They took her with them and consulted me, asked me what to do." He shook his head in disbelief. "The idiots."

"First, I was furious. Their orders were not to cause general mayhem, but only to destroy the findings of your survey, for whatever they might have been worth, but these are not educated men, Mr. Franklin. These are not even stupid men. However!" he said, holding a finger up for emphasis like an empassioned minister, "these are loyal men. When they saw your headquarters room they were confused. Which was the survey? What is a survey, anyway? What does a computer tape look like, the transparent stuff with stickum on one side? Should they look for papers with numbers? In their ignorance, they made a decision, a stupid, unnecessary decision, but a loyal one: They destroyed everything, to make certain.

"If there is any blame, in a sense it's mine. I employed these men for their dedication and overlooked their lack of intelligence." He smiled, almost apologetically. "You appreciate, I know, that this line of work doesn't attact men of the same mental capacity as your own."

"To hell with computers and surveys!" I burst out. "We're talking about a young girl whose death these buffoons are responsible for. Can we talk about that, please. Let's get to the point."

"Softly," he ordered. "Gently. We're getting there. My way. They took the girl with them, as I have said. To a cabin, a hunting lodge. They were to release her after the local primaries were over. Until then, I wanted no chance of anyone pointing a finger to say that organized criminals were out to defeat John McGrath. Organized criminals!"

he repeated scornfully. "As distinct from disorganized criminals like politicians, I suppose. But stupid men drink too much. The little girl got away while they were senseless. They had taken her shoes and her outerwear, but she was a brave young thing, and she got away anyway. The rest you know, or you've figured out for yourself. She had no idea where she was, and she died in the woods, hopelessly lost. Pity."

"Pity? The hell with pity! What are you going to do about it, that's what I want to know. Screw pity! They killed her, those two, a young girl who did nothing to them or to you. They plain killed her."

"No." His open hand slammed down on his thigh. "No. They're responsible for her death, but kill her—no. It was an accident, a preventable accident, I grant you, but I stand by my men. Where would I be if I didn't? Like every other business, I run mine on trust. I wouldn't last a week if I let my boys down like that."

All manner of responses bubbled up, such as inquiring what would be so bad if his business, as he called it, didn't last a week, but giving vent to that would have made me as stupid as Pete and Joe. Instead, I said, "Let me ask you something. Why the devil did you bring me down here, to give me a lecture on business ethics, for God's sake? What do you want from me?"

LeGrand beamed his approval. "I admire a man who keeps his eye on the main point. But we'll have to do this my way, the old-fashioned way. Don't worry, all in good time. We'll get there. I sense a certain"—his hand described circles as he searched for the word; a star sapphire flashed a couple of winks in my direction "—a certain disapproval in your tone. Good! You stick to your principles. I'll stay with mine. It may surprise you to hear it, but no sane man in my line approves of unnecessary killing as a normal procedure. It's dangerous, it makes trouble, and yes, even by our standards, it's immoral. Not to say illegal, though that may be a side issue. When I was starting out I was responsible for perhaps two deaths." He screwed up his face thoughtfully. "Three at the most, depending on how you look at it, but that was my training period, my apprenticeship, Mr. Franklin, and I had to do things I didn't like. Notice I don't say I didn't approve of it, only that I didn't like it.

"I've heard a little about your line of work, too, Mr. Franklin. When you were beginning, didn't you sometimes have to go out on the street and lie to people? Haven't I heard that people like you invite others to watch the new season's television premieres in your studios, and to give you their opinions of the shows? And haven't I heard that when you get them in their seats, you may show them the pilot film of a show so bad it's being dropped, and that you sandwich into it perhaps a dozen or more commercials, which is all you actually want to get reactions to? Isn't this lying? Isn't this deceitful? Isn't this," and he jabbed a finger at me, "corrupt?"

No college sophomore could have sneered more sincerely at the ethics of capitalism in general and advertising in particular. The only place to begin my answer was, under the circumstances, nowhere. "Yes," I replied, "it's corrupt. And if the lecture's over, can we go on?"

"Of course. Now we get to the point. In your world you need such corruption. In mine, I will not tolerate it. The other information you supplied on my men, is, from a business point of view, more serious, though I don't belittle the matter of the girl. You say they were blackmailing young George McGrath, doing a little business on the side without me knowing. How could they be doing this, Mr. Franklin? And what makes you so sure they weren't acting on my orders?"

I felt a rush of excitement. The man found my story of his lieutenants' responsibility for a young girl's death regrettable but not reprehensible. But corruption, whether in advertising or within his own ranks was too terrible a crime to be overlooked. I felt like a prospector looking for oil who finds he has to settle for gold instead. "Ah, yes," I said, "Pete and Joe's little scam with George McGrath. I knew they weren't acting on your orders because you told me so yourself."

"I told you? Despite my son's opinion, I'm not that senile. I doubt your story. It's getting near lunch. Would you like a drink while we talk about this?"

"I would, please. A martini on the rocks, if you've got the makings. Vodka, if possible. With a twist." I was drunk already with the smell of success. I grew even bolder. "And I wouldn't say no to one of your Cuban cigars, either, if I may."

"A pleasure. And now, you can begin."

"Here goes, then. You remember the last time we met I thought George was paying you to smear his father. You laughed. You said you don't do business retail, something like that. You thought the idea was very funny, the McGrath boy having anything to do with what was going on. That's how I knew your men were doing a little business on the side that you knew nothing about."

"You're not being clear. Don't play games with me about serious matters."

"Right. But first, let me ask you a question. Why did you drag a scatterbrain like Della DeGraaf out to wave a gun at John McGrath? You must have known that the garbage she slung around was so far out it couldn't come near to sticking. Or did you? I mean, why bother, when there was no point to it? Or was it the other way around? Maybe you expected—I'll bet you a box of those Cuban cigars you did—a flood of room clerks, waiters, bartenders, God knows who, to turn up with stories about seeing McGrath and that freak rolling around the gutters in Los Angeles. Didn't you even wonder where they were, why you couldn't turn them up? Weren't your West Coast people supposed to turn them up?"

My case hung on his reaction. I knew what Eileen had told me about mistakes being made, but Eileen, by her own admission, had been pushed off the controls once her usefulness was over. There had to be things she only could guess at, things she'd never have known for certain. One answer from LeGrand and I had Pete and Joe where I wanted them; another answer and those two might have me where they'd be only too delighted for words, if those freaks had any words, which in itself was a doubtful proposition.

His response was to step up to the bar and pour another drink. He did not offer me one, though my glass was empty. No candy for a bad boy? "That, Mr. Franklin," he said too mildly, "is something I will be looking into more thoroughly once I'm out from under the New Hampshire campaign. Somebody will know the answer to your question," he said with dreamy anticipation. "Somebody will tell us both where those waiters and bartenders were, the ones who, I was assured, had seen McGrath and that ridiculous creature together."

"Yes, Mr. LeGrand, I know. But *which* McGrath?"

From the cracks on his face I learned that Pierre LeGrand's puzzle muscles weren't normally in everyday use, and somewhere along the way they had atrophied. His head tilted slightly to one side, and his lips were slightly parted. He looked like a high school freshman who doesn't know the answer to the assignment. He looked ordinary; another idol down the drain. "Explain yourself," he ordered.

"The way I hear it, and from the chump himself, it's *George* McGrath the girl was wound up and pointed at. His sister even told me that; the introduction was set up at her house. George and the girl were the couple those waiters and bartenders saw. Not John, my friend."

He left the bar and sat behind his desk, slamming the drink down hard. I hoped it wouldn't leave a ring on that expensive surface. He flipped a switch. "Get me Pete and Joe. Right away."

"I think it would be better if you asked them to wait outside until you hear the rest of what I have to say," I suggested. Very timidly.

He nodded brusquely and flipped the switch again. "Never mind about the boys." Turning back to me, he nodded again. "Go on."

I cleared my throat. "You sent those two out to the Coast to take the DeGraaf girl to Iowa and have her go into her act. They took the gun with them from Boston." I wanted to ask how you get a gun on a domestic flight these days, but the man's business secrets were a side issue; no point in being pushy. "So far as you and your boys knew, Della had been lurching around town with John McGrath, and he was about to learn that the price was higher than steak, french fries, and wine for two. Somewhere along the line, and I don't know where, your boys found out the truth. My guess would be that a mistake like that couldn't last very long, and it was straightened out right after they got to L.A. to pick up Della.

"I'd say they decided to go ahead with the plan the way you told them, and not say anything to you about what they'd found out, and I'd guess it was Pete who came up with that idea. Then they could lean on George for a little pocket money if he wanted to keep them quiet. The kid was probably afraid of being landed in another mess, so he went along. Are you still with me?"

He dipped his chin about an inch and said, "Keep going."

"Well, all they had to do then was make up some story for Della, which couldn't have been too hard. They probably told her she had to discredit the father, and once he gave up on the nomination he wouldn't give a damn if the wicked witch of the west turned up as his daughter-in-law. And then they had that extra bait for her: If this fell through but she was a good girl, she'd get to be the belle of the South Side of Chicago.

"They were pretty shrewd, at least Pete was, but, as you say yourself, not too bright, and they never realized that the story would fizzle after the first flurry of scandal, because there wasn't a shred of evidence that could be turned up to keep it churning. But even after it died, they still fingered George here in the East. Probably this time they told him there'd be stories about father and son sharing the same trick, maybe as an economy measure. Hell, with all that was going on, how could the poor dummy know they'd never be able to do anything like that? It was a natural setup. What George did know for damn sure was that he was still in it up to the kazoo, and he was afraid somebody would find out, use it to hurt his father. So he paid. Maybe he didn't have much, but whatever he had, well, what the devil, it paid the bar bill. And if I know your boy Pete, it was fun. Good, dirty fun."

I stopped. But LeGrand didn't start. I asked, "What do you think?"

"I don't think. I find out."

"And when you find out?"

"Then we'll see." He shook his head. "But for now, you're wrong. Most of this you've made up. Guesswork. Pete and Joe, my boys, would never do that to me. Never do that to the organization. If they knew we had the DeGraaf girl tied into the wrong McGrath, they would have told me. They'd know it was important. They'd know I don't tolerate corruption. If there was corruption. If you're right. These are serious charges, and the consequences could be likewise for Pete and Joe. Or for you, Mr. Franklin." An avenging angel looked at me, hard and calculating.

I sat back in the chair. Not wanting to meet the man's eyes, I turned my own toward the window. The day that had begun so bright and clear in New Hampshire had collapsed down on itself like a subcompact under an overturned tractor trailer. It was dark, and a dismal scattering of snow was drifting down toward the desperation of the Boston slums. I shifted my gaze back to the equally chilly prospect of Pierre LeGrand's impassive face, and I saw an ice sculpture that would have looked more at home on the street outside.

I hoisted my ego back into fighting position, despite its silent protestations, and said, "I'm right, and you can bank on that. Let's leave out what I'm not sure of and stick to what I know for a dead certainty. That's two things: First, Della DeGraaf was pointed at the candidate's son by the people on the Coast. They turned her motor on for George, not his father. Second, I saw the boy, saw him myself, with my own eyes, paying off your boys. Not once, but twice." Another of those little white lies if I wasn't supposed to count Pete latching onto the change from George's bill in the bar as a genuine payoff. "Sure, the money wasn't in envelopes labeled 'Payoff for Pete and Joe for not snitching about Della and me,' but what do you think? You think George and the boys had a bet about how many pieces of candy there were in the jar in the window of the Rite-Aid drugstore on Fifth and Main? What do you think?"

"That's a question you keep repeating: What do I think. All right, I'll let you have your answer. It doesn't matter if the boys found a way to make money on the side, but if that means they kept back necessary information, they'll find that money cost them more than it was worth. Consequences. Justice."

His face returned to life as he warmed to the subject. The ice sculpture was gone, not melted, but transformed into something equally hard, something with cutting edges, something like finely honed steel. "I think perhaps in that case the boys would find their consciences would be bothering them. They might even come forward and confess that they were responsible for that poor girl's death. Her accidental death; these boys are still useful to me. Involuntary manslaughter, I think. They met in the motel lobby and asked her out for a drink. The three of them had too much and ended up in the cabin in the woods. They don't remember anything else. The prosecution would raise the strong presumption that she had been held involuntarily, that they took away her coat and her shoes. Two years with good behavior. Something like that."

"You seem pretty sure." I was pretty sure of something else myself, but I wasn't about to tell this old bird what it was. I sensed a chance to fix those two hoods more completely than I had ever dared hope.

"Of course. My single biggest expense is lawyers, but it's worth it. Never try to save money on legal expenses, Mr. Franklin." The kindly old grandpa, full of advice, was back in stride.

"I'll keep it in mind."

"But," he said sharply, "if you are wrong, if your story is pure fiction, as I think it is, then there would still be consequences, but of a different nature." He smiled, an even-handed disciplinarian, a stern but loving father.

"Such as?"

"Why, let's say I'd consult Pete and Joe about that. It could be I'd let them decide. After all, the crucial part of your elaborate story is that Pete and Joe held back vital information from me about the girl and young George McGrath. But you have no evidence, only supposition." He held up a hand to cut off my objections. "I know. It takes only a phone call to the Coast to find out, but that's for me to decide. Me, Mr. Franklin. But if I do, you'll be among the first to know, I can promise you that." He stood. "Enough speculation. It's making me hungry. Time for me to send you back to Manchester."

I stood too. "My bag is in your car. I'd prefer to catch the shuttle to New York."

"Good. We'll get you to the airport." He turned on the intercom. "Tell Pete I need him to drive Mr. Franklin out to Logan. Now." Turning back to me, he said, chuckling like Santa Claus, "You and Pete can talk things over on the way. Man to man."

Pete rapped on the door and came in. LeGrand, still amused at his own wit and charm, said, "Pete, take Mr. Franklin to the airport, and then I want to see you."

Pete didn't like that. "Boss, this one's a pain in the ass. Couldn't he get out there by himself? I'll spring for the cab, I have to." He looked at me. "Whatta we gotta kiss ass for, anyway, this guy?"

LeGrand's words found a path through lips that barely moved. "Because I say so," he explained with a gentle smile. "Besides, maybe you can learn something from Mr. Franklin. He's an educated man. Ask him what he knows. Learn, learn, Pete, it'll do you good, maybe. Talk to the man." Nothing compares to a comic with a sense of his own worth, and his shoulders shook again in self-appreciation, even increasing in intensity when he saw the pained expression on my face. "Goodbye, goodbye, pleasant trip."

He continued to chuckle as he shook my hand and ushered me out, still the jolly elf into whom Dr. Frankenstein has mistakenly inserted that criminal brain. I heard him laughing as I went down through the bar, Pete trailing reluctantly behind me. I heard him laughing in the car on the way to the airport. When I looked at Pete's hands on the wheel I saw two large and meaty objects that frequently come in five pound cans labelled Armour and Swift, and I heard LeGrand laughing again.

"Okay, you," Pete said, while we were waiting for a light, "the boss said you could learn me something. So speak something smart." He turned toward the back and looked at me with contempt.

"Well, look, you—"

"Ah, shaddap!" We moved forward again. "That's enough outa you, and I didn't learn from shit!" Pete was pleased with that exchange; honor had been satisfied; I had been put in my place, which was down. He even laughed a little, possibly in emulation of his employer.

When both gales of merriment died down, the one in my ears and the one in my mind, I had time to appreciate what that sly old devil in Boston had found so funny. If his men were responsible for Barbara Jellthrop's death, it was unfortunate, but it had happened in the line of duty. Stupidity would not be counted as a crime. No punishment. A reprimand perhaps, a wagging finger, an order to stand in the corner. But if they had cheated the organization, it was worse than what the law calls a crime; they would have been corrupt. Then they would be punished—but the punishment would derive from the girl's death. The law would be satisfied, though for the wrong reasons; LeGrand would be satisfied for the right reasons; and I—I could be satisfied or not, as I damn well pleased.

I might have started laughing myself if I hadn't gone hot, cold, and clammy at the same time. And of course I knew something LeGrand didn't know, something I had neglected to point out when he was sketching the scenario for punishing the boys if it turned out they had let him down. A snotty kid's chant came into my mind as I stuck my mental tongue out at the old crook: "I-know-something-YOU-don't-knowwwwww; Yah-yah-yah-yah-YAH-yah-yahhhhh."

We screeched up to the airport, Pete slamming on the brakes, probably to see if he could pitch me forward and mash my skull on the partition between us. "Thanks a bunch, James," I said, hopping out nimbly with my bag. "You can go back now and take your afternoon nap. But only after you get the Gravy Train stains off your muzzle."

Then it was my turn to laugh for real, though I'll be the first to admit I ducked into the terminal building more rapidly than the flight schedule would have required.

TWENTY-SIX

The affair had more false endings and codas than a Beethoven symphony at the master's sneakiest.

To begin with, two days later the primary results were in. McGrath, as we knew he would, had failed to get his second place, though by a mere couple of hundred votes. Then there was something about a snow storm holding up ballots, followed by the caveat that the absentee ballots hadn't been counted. After that came those pro forma demands for a recount that enlighten nothing except public awareness of the loser's fighting spirit—never say die—and lead to nothing, except this time it did, and McGrath took that second place by 153 votes.

Since that shoved Leich down to number three position, it was his turn to never say die, which he did, and at great length, which set another recount into motion. McGrath took that one too, and by an even larger margin—172 votes.

That did it. That gave our Johnny what he was after. If he could keep it up in the rest of the country, and the possibility of the bandwagon effect setting in to line up more votes on his side made that look like a reasonable goal, he'd be a party power in four years' time. Havemeyer would be landed with the loser's label in this year's election. That would make Johnny the party's fair-haired boy next time around. So Finch, Rowan, & Hyde, with Gold, Toscani, and me running interference, had done the job. Hurray, or so I foolishly thought.

I went to Ed Jorgensen and asked for a raise, naturally. Equally naturally, he pointed out with sweet reason that the candidate had made a virtue of firing his pollster; in fact, he had used it as a device to get votes. Consequently, his pollster—me—had nothing to do with the triumph. The raise was turned down. I objected, and pointed out, with what I foolishly thought was irrefutable logic, that it was my idea in the first place for him to fire me and run up and down denouncing pollsters. I demanded a recount. I got it, but I lost again, though only by one vote, Jorgensen's. I said, yeah, but the agency was sure to get the big account in four years. Nothing but fair, always the decent man, Jorgensen conceded the logic of my argument, but I was sensible enough not to ask for another recount because something told me I'd lose again.

I swallowed my frustration, but only for a short time. Let no one say that Ev Franklin can be beat up on like that without it rousing him to battle. However, being nobody's fool, I didn't set out to clobber Jorgensen, but turned on someone else instead. Eileen McGrath. I called her, and I let her know that I was still deeply offended by what she had tried to do to her father, but, I told her, I would keep her dirty secret provided she a) worked to help her father during the rest of the campaign for the party's nomination, and b) went and stayed at least a month in Missouri with her mother and her grandfather. She did a), and she did b).

George, all the nobility drained from that flabby frame by the drama in New Hampshire, restored the balance by getting himself arrested for speeding in Georgia. He claimed he was caught in a speed trap, and since his car had New York plates, it could even have been true.

The days began to lengthen. Easter was in the middle distance. I became aware of the passage of time; my own days were, if anything, growing shorter. Out of nowhere I said to Jane, "Haven't you always wanted to go to New Orleans for Mardi Gras?"

"No," she answered, "I haven't. In fact, absolutely not. I'm past the age for all that. Why?"

I ignored her touching reluctance to lower the family bank balance. "I don't see why we should keep putting it off and putting it off for one stupid reason or another until we're too old for it, do you?"

"As a matter of fact, yes, I do. Why?"

"'Cause I think we ought to go. How about it? Dinner at Antoine's? Breakfast at Brennan's?"

"Oh, for heaven's sake, Ev, all that rich food! You *know* you'd only be up half the night. You can't even hardly eat Jell-O if it's got whipped cream on it! Act your age. Besides, you really want to use up perfectly good vacation time for that?"

"You're a doll, Jane, and you're right: We won't charge it to vacation time. I run this damned department, don't I? Nobody'll ever know. Jorgensen'll be in Bermuda like every year, so who's to find out?"

Great exaggerated sighs. "Yes, dear."

We went. I was awake most of three nights running with heartburn. And I do mean running. I still say it couldn't have been the food, because the way I look at it, sauces with heavy cream should be soothing to the stomach, not upsetting. I think it must have been the water. The tea and dry toast I subsisted on were the high point of my trip, though Jane tells me the floats and the costumes down there in the streets were little short of fabulous. In fact, she talked about them for months.

More time passed, and I thought the last of my adventure was behind me. The apple trees came into bloom, and there was a late frost, but since only the McIntosh were hurt, I couldn't get too concerned. I don't like them much, anyway. The major excitement of early spring was that the wrens who had dispossessed the purple martins from a house I had erected for the exclusive use of the latter were in turn spooked off the premises by the arrival of a great crested flycatcher.

But there was one more chord ground out in June by some celestial orchestra, in the form of a clipping from the *Boston Globe*. It came in the mail; no note attached. It said that two men had turned themselves in in connection with the mysterious death of a young girl in the woods of southern New Hampshire. Their consciences had been keeping them awake nights before they made their decision to confess, and now they claimed to be at peace with themselves. There was nothing about their having joined the ranks of the born-again, that gambit apparently reserved these days for classier crooks. From the complimentary remarks attributed to the local district attorney's office I suspected that the D. A. himself was tripping down to the jailhouse to make sure they got their hot cocoa and cookies at bedtime every night. As a wise man in Boston once observed, it's foolish to economize on legal expenses.

I took out a subscription to the *Globe,* and followed the case. As LeGrand had outlined the scenario, Pete and Joe told their story about the two of them plus Barbara Jellthrop drinking too much and passing out in the cabin in the woods. The next thing they knew was that the girl was gone, while her coat and hat and gloves and shoes stayed behind. Poor girl! They were prostrate with remorse.

However, as I had so carefully neglected to mention to LeGrand, the autopsy showed no traces of alcohol or drugs in Barbara's body, a fact that the prosecution pointed out in pardonable puzzlement. Was there some other, more reasonable explanation, like kidnaping? To paraphrase the poet, the best laid plans of beasts, not men, can so easily gang aglee, whatever that may mean.

There wasn't much that could be proved one way or the other except that their first story was a lie, and they ended up with ten to twelve in the pokey, not the few years LeGrand had projected. Sometimes economizing on the truth can be almost as much of a mistake as economizing on legal expenses. I didn't imagine LeGrand would keep their old jobs open for them, either, not for so long a time, anyway.

That did it. I expected that in some magic way the election would now be rinsed out of my psyche as if it were a grass stain treated with a Finch, Rowan, & Hyde client's new wonder detergent. But one worrisome spot remained. What difference would it have made if I had been able to go on working for McGrath, doing my polls and telling him what they meant? What difference would it have made if Toscani and Gold and the speechwriters and the artists and the copywriters had had the use of my findings to develop their output? Would the candidate have come in stronger, or might he even—perish the thought—have lost out entirely? Or wouldn't it have made any difference at all?

And what did the candidate himself think the answers to these questions were? If I ever lost my job on Madison Avenue, would I gain a buddy in the White House?

Now there are a couple of mysteries to be investigated, but not, I swear, as I value my income and my sanity, in that order, by me.